NEVER HAVE I EVER KISSED MY BROTHER'S BEST FRIEND

NEVER EVER LOVE BOOK 1

JULIET BARDSLEY

Snowy Wings
PUBLISHING

Never Have I Ever Kissed My Brother's Best Friend
By Juliet Bardsley

The characters and events portrayed in this book are fictitious. Any similarity to real persons, living or dead, is coincidental and not intended by the author.

Copyright © 2019 by Juliet Bardsley/Jennie K. Brown

All rights reserved.

No part of this book may be reproduced in any form or by any electronic or mechanical means, including information storage and retrieval systems, without written permission from the author, except for the use of brief quotations in a book review.

http://www.julietbardsley.com

For new releases, give-aways, and swoon-worthy freebies, become a member of Juliet's Reader's Club!

To read novella 1 in the Mount Honey Grove Romance Series, click here!

For all the lovers of swoon-worthy YA!

For new releases, give-aways, and swoon-worthy freebies, become a member of Juliet's Reader's Club!

To read more short, sweet, and swoon-worthy books by Juliet Bardsley, click here!

CHAPTER 1

The chill of fall cut through my sweater as I sat on the cold bleachers watching Cedar Oak High's varsity soccer game.

"Go, Cory!" my mom yelled from the row below. My brother looked toward her, gave a quick nod of his head, and then his gaze settled on me. In an act of typical older-brotherness, he threw his left hand to his head, making the "loser" signal with his pointer finger and thumb. I rolled my eyes at the backward "L". He could have at least used the right hand.

I wrapped two arms around myself, wishing I'd grabbed a heavier jacket before leaving the house. I should have remembered the temperature drops a solid twenty degrees in mid-October in Central Pennsylvania. It didn't help that Cedar Oaks sat in one of the deepest valleys in the state, allowing air to funnel through at near-tornado speeds.

I looked past the game and to the sideline at the

bottom of the bleachers where Gavin Mitchell, my brother's best friend since kindergarten, practiced overhead tosses with another player. I inhaled deeply and bit the side of my lip, forcing my eyes from Gavin and back to the players on the field. I didn't want to be caught in some crazed stare-fest by the group of senior girls sitting a few benches away.

But as I sat on the sideline of the soccer game—a sport that, truth be told, I didn't find that enjoyable—faux cheering on the Cedar Oaks Raiders while my teeth literally rattled, it was Gavin Mitchell who continued to have my undivided attention.

Ugh. *Why does he have to be so gorgeous? And why can't I crush on someone more available?*

"Hey! Did you just see that?" Veda, my best friend in the universe, slapped me on the shoulder.

"Ouch!" I rubbed my arm. "See what?" I was too busy staring at Gavin as he stood on the sideline, muscular arm cocked back, ready to toss the ball to another player, to notice the goal her boyfriend had just made. I clapped my hands together. "Oh, yeah," I feigned interest and tossed a few strands of blond hair behind my ear. "Score!"

"Mmm hmm." Veda narrowed her eyes at me. "You're not even paying attention to the game, Kenz." She shot me a knowing look and then got back to watching the game. *Phew*. I'd avoided yet another confess-your-love-to-Gavin conversation.

The cold of the metal bench soaked through my skinny jeans and I rethought just how much I wanted to be here when I could be holed up in the corner of my bedroom, snuggling under a cozy blanket, reading the next act of *A Midsummer Night's Dream*. Ahh. Just the thought of that brought a smile to my face.

But I couldn't miss the chance to watch Gavin work his magic on the soccer field, now could I?

I perked up as Gavin took the field for the last two minutes of the game. And in those two minutes, the Cedar Oaks Raiders scored two more goals, beating the Millvale Trojans.

"Woohoo!" Veda cheered, jumping up from her seat. She grabbed my hand and pulled me down the bleachers with her. I struggled to keep up as she dragged me along and out on the field, but then promptly released the sleeve of my sweater to give a congratulatory hug to her boyfriend, Noah Paige.

I stood there abandoned on the sideline, awkwardly pushing my toe into the damp grass.

Suddenly I felt a hand ruffle the top of my blond head of hair, causing a few pieces to fall in my eyes. Probably Cor—

"Hey, Kenzie," the voice belonging to the hand said, and it didn't belong to my brother.

I turned to see Gavin Mitchell standing beside me. I fiddled with the hem of my jacket. "Oh, hey, Gavin!" I awkwardly raised my hand to give him a high five, but he looked away as my brother tossed him his water bottle. Gavin caught it perfectly. I sighed inside. Swoon. Everything about Gavin was perfect. From the way he squeezed the bottle so a steady stream of water gushed into his mouth, to the way he pushed a hand through his sandy-brown hair so that a few pieces curled perfectly around his right ear.

"What?" Gavin flicked a finger to his earlobe. "Something on my face?"

I closed my gaping mouth, caught in the stare, and then swallowed hard. "No ... uh ... great game!" I raised my hand again and awkwardly tapped him on the shoulder. As soon as I did it, I regretted the decision. Gavin squinted and looked at me like he always did—as the annoying, awkward little sister of his best friend.

Cory gave me the side-eye and then spoke to Gavin. "Great game, man," he said. They did one of those bro handshake-slash-half-hugs. "We're heading to Oaks Diner if you wanna come?" Cory looked over my head and to Gavin as he spoke. I bowed out and turned my back from them, knowing the invite wasn't intended for me. But just before I reached Veda who'd finally unlatched from Noah, I heard Gavin speak. "You coming?"

My heart hammered against my chest. "Sure!" I said quickly, pivoting.

Cory scrunched his face. "He was talking to Noah."

I looked to my right where Noah stood.

"Oh." My face grew hot with embarrassment, and I was sure my naturally rosy cheeks flamed a vibrant shade of cherry red. "I ... uh ..."

"You're such a spaz." Cory punched a fist into my shoulder. "Thanks for coming to the game, little sis!" He gave me a condescending pat on the head and then ran to the bleachers where Mom waited with a grin.

Just before I turned, Gavin caught my eye and gave a small shoulder shrug. "Sorry," he mouthed.

Great. Now he could add pitiful to the list of qualities he surely saw in me.

I threw my head back in defeat as Gavin walked, no, more like sauntered, away from me, his sweaty jersey clinging to his back so the muscles showed underneath.

Sigh.

Veda sucked some air between her teeth and spoke. "Ouch."

I stared straight ahead and watched as Gavin jumped into his Jeep Wrangler. "Why *am* I such a total spaz around him?"

Veda nudged my shoulder with hers. "You need to either get over your Gavin crush, Kenz." She rolled her eyes. "Or tell him how you feel."

I sighed. Veda had been my best friend since fourth grade when we bonded over monkey bars on the playground. She was the only person in the world to know the truth about my feelings for Gavin Mitchell. And no matter how much I tried to get over my obsession with him or tell him how I felt, I couldn't get over one fact.

I was in love with Gavin Mitchell, and I'd been in love with him since the eighth grade.

CHAPTER 2

There was nothing worse than the smell of Mr. Fretz's English class. I was pretty sure his breakfast consisted of a not-so-fresh tuna sandwich, burnt toast, and an overly strong cup of coffee. Mr. Fretz passed by and slapped the latest quiz on my desk. "See me after class," he whispered. *Definitely old coffee*, I thought as his breath lingered in the two-foot space around my head.

I flipped the paper over and sighed. Yet another D-minus. After the game last night, I'd skipped out on the victory celebration at the diner, opting instead to study for the quiz on Act 2 of Shakespeare's *A Midsummer Night's Dream*. I looked at the sea of red *X's* on my paper and huffed. Obviously didn't study enough.

I turned around to see a similar grade on Emma Good's quiz, which she promptly pulled away from my gaze, and then I inconspicuously glanced over the shoulder in front of me to see the grade on Kenzie's quiz. Yet another A. Figures.

As much crap as Cory gives his sister for being a nerd, it looked like she was in better shape of passing old Fretz's British literature class than I was. And she was only a junior.

"Pssst," I hissed just as Mr. Fretz made his way down the aisle, but his head whipped around just as I did it. I closed my mouth, sat up straight, and pretended to study the bloodbath of a quiz in front of me. The last thing I needed was a detention for unnecessary chatter from the teacher with Cedar Oaks High's highest record of detention assignments.

I looked toward Kenzie's quiz again, and then let my eyes settle on the back of her head. *When did she start wearing her hair straight?*

As if Kenzie felt my gaze, she pivoted her head toward me. Her green eyes that looked emerald-like against her purple scarf, met mine and wrinkled in the corners as she sent a half-smile my way.

I opened my mouth to say something just as Mr. Fretz spoke. "I want to focus on the unique rhythm of Shakespeare's works," he began. "Now, as I recite the opening of the play"—Mr. Fretz paused and pointed to lines he'd written on the front board—"tap your hand on your desk in the rhythm of a heartbeat. Dah *Dum* Dah *Dum* Dah *Dum*."

I tapped along with the rest of the class and zoned out as Mr. Fretz droned on about something called iambic pentameter. Whatever that was. I had other things to think about—like how I was going to pull a passing grade in my worst subject to stay eligible for soccer playoffs.

In front of me, Kenzie stole a look over her shoulder and nodded toward my hand. I jerked it away from my desk, realizing nobody else tapped along anymore, and I'd just done my first iambic pentameter solo.

Mr. Fretz stood over me. "Pray tell, Mr. Mitchell. Art thou attention paying?"

The class giggled as he looked over his black-framed glasses and studied my face. But one person wasn't giggling—Kenzie.

I stared up at Mr. Fretz and at the furry toupee that sat atop his head. Even if I wasn't well versed in Shakespeare, I knew what he asked didn't make much sense. "Well ... I." I cleared my throat. "I just thought that maybe—." As I opened my mouth to say more, the shrill buzzing sound of the intercom rang out through the class.

"Would Gavin Mitchell please report to the athletic director's office. Gavin Mitchell. To the A.D.'s office."

Saved by the intercom.

I grabbed my books, shoved my quiz in my bag, and hustled out of the room. I couldn't get out of Brit Lit fast enough.

* * *

Coach Temple, Cedar Oaks High's Athletic Director, who also happened to be the head soccer coach, sat on the other side of his large wooden desk, his fingertips playing with the edges of his graying mustache. He leaned back in his chair and crossed his arms over his chest.

"Look, Mitchell. You know I've done things in the past to get you through classes." He cleared his throat and leaned toward me. "To keep you eligible," he whispered.

I nodded, remembering the strings Coach Temple pulled with my junior-year English teacher. I had to clean Miss Bonfanti's whiteboards for three weeks straight to get my D to a solid C-minus. Although not the scholarly way to bring up a grade, it worked well enough for me to play through the end of the season.

"Things don't work that way with ol' Fretzie," Coach admitted, almost as if he read the thought from my head. He put his hands in the air. "So I'm afraid that in order for you to be eligible for playoffs, you'll need to take your studying seriously."

I sighed. "I do, Coach. It's just English and me have never gotten along."

And that wasn't an exaggeration. It was no secret I didn't have the best record with reading and then actually retaining information. I'm a visual learner. I mean, it took me watching the movie version of *To Kill A Mockingbird to* realize the narrator, Scout, was actually a girl and not a little boy. Then there was *Romeo and Juliet*. I didn't realize Nurse wasn't actually a real medical nurse, but Juliet's caretaker, until the end of Act 2. Thank goodness we watched the 1960s version in class to get that straight.

But I also knew that only watching the movie wasn't enough for Fretz's class.

Coach Temple fumbled with his computer mouse and clicked around on the screen. "I know Principal Pence sent a list of peer tutors at the beginning of the year," he muttered.

I swallowed hard. A peer tutor? The last thing I wanted to do in my extra time was be holed up with some smart kid who'd just make me feel dumber than I actually am. "I think I can manage on my own." I grabbed my bag to leave.

"Oh no, you don't." Coach narrowed his eyes. "If you aren't on that field then I'll have to play Michael Sands."

I cringed at the mention of Michael's name. He'd wanted my position on the soccer team for the past three years.

Coach clasped his hands together. "Plus, how's the whole *managing on your own* been working out for you?"

I shrugged and felt the D-minus quiz burning a hole in my backpack. "Point taken."

"We need you on the field, Mitchell. Playoffs start in seven days and I happen to know a few scouts will be in the crowd taking notes."

I sat up straighter. "From Penn State?"

"That's information I can't say for certain." Coached winked, confirming it was right.

Playing soccer for Penn State would be a dream come true; something I wanted ever since age five when I slipped my feet into my first pair of black and neon-green cleats. "Alright."

Coach smiled. "Then it's settled. Tutoring it is." He double-clicked on a file and a list of names popped up on his screen. "Now we need someone whose schedule is pretty open and who currently has an A in class."

I impatiently tapped my Converse on the floor below as Coach clicked through student grades and schedules.

"Claire Mullins has a high B."

I rolled my eyes. I'd broken up with Claire a month ago, and the last thing I needed was for her to think there was a chance of getting back together. "That's a hard pass."

Coach moved the cursor down the list. "Ah!" His beady eyes lit up as he scanned over the screen. "This one. She has a solid ninety-eight percent and no other after-school commitments"—he paused and snorted—"besides writing for the literary magazine."

I actually read the latest edition of the literary magazine, *Ampersand*, it wasn't half bad. But I ignored Coach's grumble and sat on the edge of my chair to get a better look. "So who is it?"

Coach Temple squinted at the name and then spoke. "Mackenzie Fair, English extraordinaire." He laughed at his own horrible attempt at rhyme.

"Cory's little sister."

"She's already in a twelfth-grade course?"

I shrugged. "She's always been smart." I remember Cory complaining about him having to take all English classes while his sister skipped ahead. "Skipped English 9."

"Is that so?" He stood from his chair and walked toward the office door. "I'll talk to Mr. Fretz and set up the first session for after school today."

I tossed my bag over my shoulder. "But what about practice?"

Coach frowned. "Well ... I do need you there. I'll say something to Fretz about finding an alternate time." He shrugged. "Since she's Cory's sister, maybe you can just study at her house?"

"Got it." I headed toward the door, but just as I reached the knob, Coach spoke again.

"Oh, and Gavin?"

"Yes, sir?"

He cocked an eyebrow. "Don't forget you'll need to be working, not flirting."

I huffed. Mackenzie Fair was my best friend's little sister. "Oh ... I don't think it will be a problem."

CHAPTER 3

"I can't do it," I said adamantly to Vera and then took a sip of my chai latte. At the end of school today, Mr. Fretz called me into his classroom and told me I had my first English tutoring pupil of the year—Gavin Mitchell. I wanted to be excited, but that was a bit hard when all I could do around him was act like an utter spaz. "I can barely handle sitting in front of Gavin in class. How do you expect me to be alone with him? One-on-one?"

Veda and I sat at our home away from home, Cafe Prose, a coffee shop slash used bookstore in the center of Cedar Oaks town square. We were poised on stools at the coffee bar, sipping on chai lattes and munching on pumpkin muffins. Veda took a bite of her muffin and spoke through chews. "Well, hasn't he been around you pretty much your entire life?"

"Ha!" I practically spat out my drink. "If you consider playing hide-and-seek as kids and his effectively ignoring me anytime he comes over to my house to hang out with Cory, then sure." I wrapped my hands around my mug to warm them up. "Besides, he hasn't said more than a 'hey, Mac' or 'hi, Kenzie' these past few years. He usually picks up Cory, and then they're off to soccer practice or a party to no doubt flirt with hot senior girls."

"Is that really how you think all boys spend their time?" She pursed her lips at me. "Anyway, this is your chance, Kenz." Veda clinked her mug with mine and then shimmied her shoulders. "I can already see it. You start out by tutoring him. Then you confess your three-year, undying love for him." She placed a dramatic hand to her forehead. "And then he sees you as more than his friend's sister. After that you have your first kiss. And then you date all the way through college and live happily ever after. White picket fence. Two kids and a dog. Yada, yada, yada." She giggled.

I flicked a wrist at Veda. "I think you've been reading too many romance novels."

"No." She laughed. "I've been watching too many Hallmark movies with my mom." Veda cleared her throat and her voice turned serious. "For real though, Kenz. You should do it." She leaned back in her chair. "If you don't, I know you'll regret it."

I set down my mug and narrowed my eyes. "*If* I decided to do this. And that's a big if—."

"*When* you decide do it." She stuck a finger in my face. "If you don't agree to this, then I might be inclined to let a few things slip to Noah." She hid a mischievous smirk behind her mug and a few pieces of dark brown hair fell in her face. She pushed them away with the back of her hand, her many bangles clinking and clanking against her mug. "And you know how all that locker room talk spreads ..."

"You wouldn't!" I reached for the muffin in the middle of the table, but Veda slid the plate away.

She looked me in the eye. "Oh, I would." The way her lips pursed and eyebrows raised told me she was serious.

I relented. "Fine."

Veda smirked and then picked up her phone.

"What are you doing?" I asked.

She shoved the last bite of muffin in her mouth and tapped her fingers to the phone. "Just letting Noah know the Cedar Oaks' starting striker will be eligible for play-offs in no time."

Two minutes later, Noah had texted Gavin. And not thirty seconds after that, a text popped up on my phone.

Hey its Gavin. I'll see you at 7. Ur place.

I nervously tapped my fingers on the handle of my mug. "I guess this is really happening."

* * *

I'D NEVER in my life put so much thought into choosing an outfit to study in. I pushed some fingers through my blond hair, an attempt to add volume to the roots, but on me it looked like I'd just stuck my finger in a live socket.

Blech. I grabbed my brush and smoothed down the strands.

"Don't be a spaz, Kenzie," I reminded myself, dabbing on some strawberry-scented lip-gloss. "It's just Gavin, and you've known him forever."

It's just Gavin. But Gavin stopped being "just Gavin" after I'd developed a crush on him right after my dad died in eighth grade. After the funeral, Mom had a reception back at the house for all the guests. It was Gavin who arrived first. It was Gavin who helped put out the food and greeted people as they came inside while Mom, Cory, and I sat stoic in the living room. It was Gavin who stuck around at the end to help Mom and me clean up afterward. And it was Gavin who'd hugged me harder than anyone else on his way out the door.

It was in that last moment, with his arms wrapped around me, pulling me close to his chest, that the more-than-my-brother's-best-friend feelings for Gavin began.

The doorbell suddenly rang, snapping me back to reality.

Mom poked her head out her office door at the end of the hall. "You getting it, Kenz?"

"Yeah," I called. I glanced at myself in the mirror and grabbed at the hem of my gray sweater, pulling it just enough so it covered the top half of my leggings. I jogged down the stairs and took a deep breath before opening the door.

"Hey, Kenzie," Gavin said, running a hand through his sandy hair. He'd changed out of his sweaty soccer uniform and into a pair of jeans and a Nike half-zip shirt.

Tucked under his arm was *A Midsummer Night's Dream* and a notebook. *Sigh.* He was even cuter with a book in his hands.

He stepped toward me and shivered. "It's kind of cold out here," he hinted.

I shook my head from side to side. "Yeah, sorry." I moved against the door so he could step around me. "Come on in."

I inhaled a blend of fresh ivory soap and pine as he stepped by.

"Hey, Muffin!" Gavin reached a hand down to pet our labradoodle. Muffin's tail wagged faster and faster as she jumped up on Gavin. He threw a head back and laughed. "Forever puppy!" He bent down to give her a scratch behind her ear, and just as I leaned over to pet her too, Gavin stood up.

"Ouch!" he yelped, his head bashing my elbow. He dropped his books to the ground and put a hand to his head.

"Oh my goodness!" I winced in vicarious pain. "I'm so sorry. I thought you were staying down there, but you weren't, and then I bent down, and..." *Stop rambling, Mackenzie.*

Gavin put his hands up in surrender. "Is it safe to stand?" He chuckled. "Let's keep the concussions on the soccer field," he teased, rubbing at the side of his head.

"Good idea." I walked toward the dining room. "Shoot."

Gavin's eyes darted from one bouquet of flowers to the next and then the next. "What's this for?"

I'd totally forgotten about the mess. Dozens of chrysanthemums and fall greenery dotted the red tablecloth. "Mom's getting things together for her new nursing home's opening, so the dining room is a makeshift flower shop right now." I shrugged. "I guess we can work in the kitchen."

I moved the centerpiece from the island and we spread out our books. Although I didn't make eye contact with Gavin, I was well aware of his presence. "So what exactly do you need help with?"

Gavin flipped through his notebook and pulled out the quiz from yesterday.

"Ouch." I passed it back to him. "That's rough."

"Tell me about it." Gavin put up two exasperated arms. "I just read this stuff and it doesn't make any sense at all."

"What part, exactly?"

Gavin looked intently at his paper. "It's just ..." he started and then his blue eyes met mine. A flicker of something I couldn't quite define crossed his face. He shook his head. "Um ... I just get confused with the characters. So Hermia likes Demetrius, but gets tricked into loving—."

"It's actually Lysander she loves."

"Huh?"

"In the beginning." I flipped to Act 1 and pointed to the passage with Hermia's father. "Hermia is in love with Lysander. But then Puck puts on the spell for Oberon and Titania."

Gavin let out a frustrating sigh. "This is ten times more confusing than *Romeo and Juliet*."

I bit the side of my lip, weighing whether or not to say what was on my mind. But Veda was right. I had to take more chances or I'd regret it. "I think I have a better idea." I closed our books. "Follow me."

CHAPTER 4

Kenzie led me to the basement where Cory and I usually hung out and played Soccer Xtreme on the Xbox.

She moved to a dusty cabinet on the back wall of the room. "We'll only watch the first two acts," she said, grabbing a DVD from a drawer. Taking me off guard, she tossed it to me with pretty accurate aim. "Only so you get the characters straight, so you know who's who moving forward."

I looked down at the title. *A Midsummer Night's Dream.* "Why do you have this?" I flipped the case over in my hands. "From 1999?"

She grabbed it from my hands and popped out the DVD. "Do you want me to help you or not?" Her other hand rested on her hip.

I narrowed my eyes, taken aback by her commanding nature. I'd obviously hit a soft spot. "I do."

She ran a hand over the case. "Dad loved Shakespeare," she muttered before placing the DVD in the Xbox console. Kenzie sat down on the plaid hand-me-down couch her and Cory's mom had picked up at a church sale.

The couch gave way under me as I sat down next to her. "Is that why you're so into it?"

Kenzie cleared her throat and her vibrant green eyes met mine. "Partly." She leaned toward me, and scents of vanilla and strawberry filled my nose as she nudged my shoulder with hers. "Plus, I'm just a huge nerd who likes watching Shakespeare for fun." She said the last sentence in a mock-Cory tone.

I opened my mouth to speak, realizing the times she'd surely been in earshot whenever her brother made fun of his bookworm of a sister—bringing novels and homework to soccer tournaments and passing up parties for weekends of studying. "I never said—."

"It's nothing." She pushed the air with the back of her hand and then grabbed the remote control. "My brother will always see me as a little kid."

I knew what she said was true. But even though Cory always saw Kenzie as his little sister, there'd been times in the past few years when I'd stopped seeing her that way, but I wasn't about to admit that to her now. "Well ..." I started, glancing at my phone. 7:45. "Should we watch it?"

Kenzie nodded slowly and pressed play. The opening credits rolled as Puck entered the screen with the opening monologue. The small horns on his head shimmered under the twinkle lights suspended from trees. I glanced over to see Kenzie's eyes fixed to the screen and a small tear glistening in the corner of her eye. She slowly wiped it away and then shifted in her seat. "Wouldn't it be crazy if it were that easy?" she whispered. "If you could sprinkle some fairy dust and the person you like, liked you back?"

I studied the side of Kenzie's face. The way her blond hair was brighter in the strands that framed her chin. How she watched with alert, emerald eyes and bit the side of her lip while she sat engrossed in the movie. I wondered if she even realized she'd just asked that aloud.

I swallowed hard. *She's my best friend's little sister.*

But in all honesty, I knew that over the past three years or so, Kenzie ceased to seem so little, so immature. She'd grown out of her braces, shot up about five inches, and lost the middle-school chubby-cheek look. Sure, she was more bookish than the girls I typically went for, but there was something innocent and endearing about Mackenzie Fair.

"What is is?" Kenzie asked, her eyes now on me.

I shifted in my seat and shook my head, shaking my thoughts about Kenzie away with it. "Nothing. Just ... um ..." Shoot. I hadn't paid attention to the entire opening of the play. "Can we actually re-watch the last few minutes again?"

Kenzie raised an eyebrow and then did that thing again where she bites the side of her lip. "Sure," she finally said.

This time, as I re-watched the movie, I paid attention, purposefully ignoring the girl sitting to my left.

* * *

"You ROCKIN' all A's yet?" Cory asked the next morning before British literature.

After I got home last night, I'd jotted down a few notes about what Kenzie and I had watched, but I couldn't get Cory's sister out of my thoughts. *Stop this, Gavin.*

I faked a yawn. "Not quite yet, but the movie helped. A lot."

Cory huffed. "Yeah, when I got home from Noah's, Mom said you and Kenzie were studying." He narrowed his eyes at me. "Now, don't you be trying anything with my little sis."

Cory had always been protective of his younger sister when it came to boys, and he had scared away a few of Mackenzie's admirers over the past two years. Let's just say, many guys at Cedar Oaks had noticed how *fair* Mackenzie Fair had gotten.

Even though I knew Cory was just messing with me now, that didn't erase the unease that prickled at my stomach. I forced an eye-roll. "Yeah, right," I finally said, brushing him off.

Cory slammed his locker shut and we walked toward our classes. "Anyway, Emma and Claire are heading to Cafe Prose after practice tonight and asked if we wanted to go along."

"I need to see how English goes before I make that call."

Cory nodded. "You bailed last nigh—."

"I had to study."

Cory slapped my hand. "Just let me know about Cafe Prose."

"Alright." I flung my backpack over my shoulder and walked into Fretz's class. Ever the studious one, Kenzie was already in her seat having a conversation Michael Sands—senior class treasurer, second striker behind me, and number-one ladies' man. He also happened to be the number-one guy she should be avoiding. For some reason, this didn't sit well with me. I leaned forward, attempting to catch part of their conversation.

I watched Michael scoot his chair closer to Kenzie. She countered with sliding her chair to the left and away from him. *Nice.* I smiled inside.

"So you know Emma's having a party this weekend?" Michael stated the obvious. The entire school knew about Emma's party.

Michael continued. "And if you wanted someone to take you ..." his voice trailed off as he drummed a few fingers on her desk, too close to her hand for comfort. "I'd be happy to do the honor. I could pick you up around eight."

I leaned in closer to hear Kenzie's response.

She moved her hand from the desk and grabbed her pen. It twisted between her fingers. "I'd have thought Michael Sands, of all people, would already be bringing some random vapid girl," she snarked.

Nice.

"Well ..." Michael stuck out his chest. "I wanted to have the most gorgeous junior at Cedar Oaks on my arm."

Kenzie's green eyes met his and then narrowed. "Well, parties really aren't my thing."

"Come on," Michael purred. Jerk sure was persistent. "I promise you it'll be fun."

Kenzie stared ahead and spoke through her teeth. "I'm gonna have to pass."

"Come on," Michael pressed. "It'll be a night you'll never forget."

Kenzie's jaw dropped as he trailed a finger down her arm.

Oh, no, he doesn't.

I reached forward and flicked his hand from her arm. "She said no, Mikey." I hoped it would stop there—no reason to make a scene.

Michael didn't drop it. He clenched and unclenched his fists. "This was a conversation between me and Mackenzie."

I stood over him. "It ceased to be a conversation when you laid a finger on her."

Michael stood next and met my infuriated gaze. "Coming to the rescue for your little girlfriend, huh?"

Kenzie stepped between us and gently placed a hand on my chest, which burned under her touch. "Cut it out, guys," she hissed. She turned to Michael. "No means no." Then her eyes met mine. "And you should calm down."

I took a step back, inhaled deeply, and then sighed. "Fine," I said, relieved to see Michael moving to his seat across the room as the rest of the class mumbled and whispered to one another. So much for not making a scene.

Just as Mr. Fretz entered the classroom to begin the latest lesson on Shakespeare, I caught Michael mouth to me, "Watch your back."

Great, ineligible and threatened. This was turning into an excellent week.

CHAPTER 5

"You need to give me *all* the details." Veda's eyes grew wide. "Right this very minute."

I put down my copy of *Pride and Prejudice* that she'd interrupted me from.

I quirked an eyebrow. "How did you know I'd be here?"

"Called your cell…"

I grabbed my phone from my bag and realized it was still on silent from school. "Yet that doesn't answer my question."

She slung her bag on the floor and stood in front of me, hands crossed over her chest. "I know how you like to come here." She gestured to my comfy chair. "Curl your feet under your butt, and do this whole reading thing all by your lonesome." She winked. "Nerd."

I put up a hand. "Repeat those last words, please."

"Nerd?"

"The ones before."

"Mmm." She scrunched her face. "By your lonesome."

"Those were the ones." I tilted my head to the side. "And yet here you are," I teased.

"Hardy, har, har." Veda took the chair next to me and leaned on the faux leather armrest, looking intently at me.

"Can I help you?" I turned my head toward her while holding the book near my face.

"So are you gonna tell me about that thing in Fretz's class today?"

My eyes grew wide as I set my book down for the second time in two minutes. "You heard about that?"

Veda frowned. "Ohhhh, I heard about it. The entire junior and senior classes heard about it."

I felt my cheeks grow warm. Of course the entire school knew about it. "Michael was out of line, and Gavin stuck up for me," I said nonchalantly. A smile instantly spread across my face at the mention of Gavin's name.

Veda pursed her lips. "Well that sounds like potential boyfriend behavior."

I ran a finger around the edge of my mug. "More like big brother's best friend behavior."

Veda reached for the latte the barista handed to her and then turned toward me. "Are you sure it's not anything more? Maybe Gavin's been madly in love with you too."

I nodded my head assuredly. "Absolutely sure it's not anything more from him."

Veda took a sip of her latte and frowned. "Maybe you're right," she muttered into her drink. "Cause he just walked in with Claire Mullins."

I turned around to see Claire with her perfectly manicured hand tucked in the crook of Gavin's arm. Gross fest. She pushed her long auburn locks behind her shoulder and giggled, leaning a head on Gavin's shoulder. He shifted under her head's weight, and I laughed inside as her head fell forward because of his move.

"Stop staring," Veda whispered and nudged my arm.

I turned my head and slunk down lower in the chair, hoping nobody except Veda noticed. "I told you he wasn't interested in me."

Veda chuckled. "They're not even together anymore."

I knew Gavin and Claire had broken up, but it was more obvious than ever by the way Claire clung to him, she wanted him back. And who wouldn't? He was athletic, gorgeous, and one of the nicest guys in Cedar Oaks.

She was the opposite; the stereotypical mean girl you watch in movies—beautiful on the outside but cruel on the inside.

Just as I went to open my mouth, I felt a hand on my shoulder. "Hey, sis." Cory stood with his hand on the back of the chair. "Aren't you uncomfortable?"

"No," I lied. My neck already ached from the awkward body scrunch I'd positioned myself in.

"Okay." Gosh, he thought I was a total weirdo. "Well,

can you tell Mom we're heading to Gavin's, so I won't be home for dinner?"

I sat up and glanced to the coffee bar where Gavin, Claire, and her best friend Emma Pierce still ordered from the barista. "Sure," I spat out as quick as possible, an attempt to get Cory away from me before he gave away my presence.

"Thanks."

Dodged that one.

"Tell me when they're gone," I spoke through clenched teeth.

Veda hid a smirk behind her vanilla latte. "Too late."

My eyes grew wide as I heard footsteps approaching.

"Kenz?" Gavin's familiar swoony voice spoke from behind.

I pushed myself up from the chair, cursing myself for ever slinking down in the first place. "Oh, hey, Gavin."

He stepped in front of me and ran a hand through his sandy hair—a gesture he did a lot, but I never tired of seeing. "I was wondering if we could talk for a minute?"

I played with the edge of my book. "Um ... yeah. That's good. That'd be fine. We can..."

Stop talking, Mackenzie.

"I need to meet up with Noah, anyway." Veda grabbed her bag, sent me a wink, and then left the coffee shop.

Suddenly I heard Claire's snarky, nasally voice from behind. "Are you coming, sweets?"

Gavin rolled his eyes and then turned toward Claire who leaned against the door.

"I'll meet up with you guys in a bit." He stole a glance over his shoulder to look at me. "I need to talk to someone."

"Just hurry it up," Claire spat.

"Someone's sure demanding," I muttered.

Murmured under my breath or not, Gavin heard. "We're not together anymore."

"Mmm." I swallowed down a smile as Gavin took the seat next to me.

"Two things." He threw two fingers in the air.

"Okay ..."

"First, I heard Fretz is planning a pop-quiz for Monday, and thought we could maybe get together this weekend for a quick study sesh?"

"Tomorrow would work," I chimed in a little too quickly. My face immediately flushed, I was sure of it.

Gavin didn't seem to notice. "Great! Would noon work?"

I warmed inside. "Perfect."

"And after that last pop-quiz, I don't think watching the movie is going to be enough for an A."

"I never said the movie is a replacement for the actual play. Think of it as a supplement to the text." I bit the side of my lip, realizing how nerdy that sounded.

Gavin laughed, unfazed. "School just comes natural to you, doesn't it?"

I played with the handle on my mug and shrugged. "I guess so."

"So the other thing ..." Gavin ran his fingers around

the edge of his to-go lid. "I wanted to see how you're doing after ..." He paused. "You know."

I took a sip of chai and then looked up at Gavin. His baby-blue eyes looked even bluer against his navy jacket, and the way he looked at me now reminded me of how he held me after Dad's funeral a few years ago. Something fierce and protective and perfect. I plastered on a smile. "I'm fine. Michael's always been a jerk."

"You can say that again. He's always hated me."

"Why?"

Gavin leaned forward in his chair and I could smell his clove-scented cologne. I wanted to melt right then and there. *Focus, Mackenzie.*

"Remember when your brother and I played in that band?" he asked.

"I remember." I giggled out loud at the ridiculous name they settled on. "Fluorescent Clowns, right?"

Gavin kicked his head back and laughed. "Yeah."

In ninth grade, Cory had decided to form a band. His plan was to make it big, play some gigs in Harrisburg and Philly, get discovered by a huge music production company, and then travel the world for the sole purpose of having girls fall at his feet. Obviously, that never panned out.

After making the rounds at middle school parties and a total of two gigs at Cafe Prose, the band broke up.

Gavin sighed. "Well, Michael and I both auditioned to play bass. I got the part over him, and he's hated me ever since."

"You're kidding me, right?" I rolled my eyes. "He hates you over *that?*"

Gavin shook his head. "Yep. It's that ridiculous. And ..."

"And what?"

Gavin leaned against the armrest, his torso turned toward me. "And he's always hated the fact I'm Coach Temple's first striker."

I pulled my lips to the side, unsure what that meant.

Gavin read my mind. "It's the most coveted position on the soccer team. And if I don't get my grade up, then Michael Sands will slip right into my position for playoffs." He tapped the side of his cup. "And if that happens, then I might as well say goodbye to a potential scholarship."

I tilted my head. "What do you mean?"

Gavin's face turned serious. "There might be a scout from Penn State at our next game, and I *need* to be on the field."

"I see." I raised my mug in the air. "Well, I'll do my best to help you." He clinked his cup with mine. "And," I added, "thanks for stepping in today. I really appreciate it."

"You don't mess with ..." Gavin paused and his eyes darted to his drink.

"You don't what?" I prompted.

He cleared his throat and a small smile curled up his cheek. "You don't mess with my best friend's little sister."

I cringed inside, his words confirming what I thought

to be true. "Right." I put the mug to my face, masking my disappointment as best I could.

Gavin stood. "I guess I'll see you tomorrow then."

I forced a smile. "Tomorrow."

Gavin walked out of the cafe, the bell above the door jingling on his way out.

"Great," I huffed.

Best friend's little sister.

CHAPTER 6

"Mitchell!" Coach yelled from across the field. I jogged over to him, my damp shirt clinging to me as the wind cut through it. Practice on these below-thirty-degree mornings was never pleasant.

But I forced out a smile. "What's up, Coach?"

Coach Temple narrowed his eyes. "Tell me how that tutoring's going?"

I shrugged. "Only had one session. Nothing to report quite yet."

Coach stepped closer to me and put a hand on my shoulder. "Just got word that a certain scout might be showing up at next Saturday's playoff game."

"No way!" I raised my eyebrows. "So it is true."

"Yes." His voice turned serious. "And Wednesday is the ineligibility cutoff for grades."

I nodded. "I'm aware, sir." That meant I only had three school days to get myself to a passing grade in

Fretz's English class or I could kiss playing in that game goodbye.

"I can't afford my number-one striker to be sitting the bench, and you can't afford not to be seen." Coach punched a fist to his other hand. "So you do whatever you have to do to get that grade up. Do you understand me?"

I swallowed. "Yes, sir."

"Fit in extra sessions with Fair's sister. Pull all-nighters. Do whatever you need to do," Coach repeated. "If I could pull Shakespeare out of his grave to teach you himself, I would."

I laughed. "That won't be necessary." I paused. "Seriously. It will be fine." I turned to get back on the field, hoping that it would.

"Oh, and Mitchell?"

I pivoted on my cleats. "Yes, Coach?"

He stepped closer to me, so if anyone were to walk by they couldn't hear his voice. "I hear what these boys say about the younger Fair. She's quite a looker."

I swallowed down a smile. I couldn't deny the fact that Mackenzie had turned into one of the most attractive girls at Cedar Oaks, even if she didn't realize it yet, and even if I shouldn't see her that way. "I know, Coach."

He frowned and then his eyes met mine. "Don't let that distract you. Your future rides on these playoffs."

I put my hands up as if in surrender. "You don't need to worry about that."

"Good to know. Good to know, son."

I shifted my weight. "Was there anything else?"

Coach slapped a hand to my shoulder. "That's all for now."

* * *

I STOOD in front of the mirror in the boys' locker room, thankful another Saturday morning of grueling soccer practice was over. Four hours, fourteen drills, and a chat with Coach Temple had me beat, but I needed to rally because I had an afternoon of studying to do.

Mr. Fretz assigned us to read Act 3 of *A Midsummer Night's Dream* this weekend, and from what I'd heard from students in his other British literature class—a class two days ahead of ours—there'd be a quiz, and not the kind of quiz you can get answers from watching the movie adaptation.

But come on? A pop-quiz on an act we're to read completely on our own—no class lecture, discussion, or handouts whatsoever?

I ran a comb through my hair. Thank goodness I had Kenzie.

A sudden warmth came over me as her name moved through my mind. Kenzie.

Stop this, Gavin.

Gosh, but did she look cute curled up in that chair in front of the fireplace at Cafe Prose yesterday. Her green eyes had peered over her glasses as she talked with me, nudging them up her nose once in a while. And I loved the way her blond hair was pinned behind her ears so I could see the pair of stud earrings she always wore—two small ruby gems her father had given her for her twelfth birthday, just a few months before his heart attack. I don't think she's taken them off since.

"Hey, man!" Cory said, jarring me from my thoughts.

"Oh, hey."

"Who are you getting pretty for?" he teased. I avoided looking at him directly, pushed a comb through my hair once more, and then tossed on a clean t-shirt and pair of jeans. For some reason, I didn't want to tell him the next item on my agenda today was studying with his sister. Even if it was innocent enough.

Cory grabbed my cologne from the counter and spritzed some over his sweatshirt. He turned the nozzle toward me and sprayed.

"Come on, man!"

He put the cologne down. "You gettin' back together with Claire?"

I forced out a laugh then tossed my dirty uniform into my gym bag. "Yeah, right."

I let out a sigh of relief when Cory moved onto a new topic. "You going to Emma's party tonight?"

I pushed a hand through my hair and sighed. "I think so."

Cory slapped a hand to mine and then patted me on the back. "Nice. I'm heading over early to help Emma out, so we'll just meet you there."

"Sounds good, man."

I grabbed my game bag and headed out to my Jeep. Just as I turned it on, my back pocket vibrated with a text.

My heart picked up speed when I saw the name flash across my screen.

Mackenzie: Change of plans. Helping my mom at new retirement home. We need to reschedule, unless you want to study between setting stuff up ;)

I frowned, disappointed for two reasons. One—after reading Act 3 last night and being completely lost, I needed the tutoring session today. Maybe even another one tomorrow.

And two—something pricked at my stomach at the thought of seeing Mackenzie.

I shook that thought from my head.

You don't have a thing for Cory's sister.

You can't have a thing for Mackenzie Fair.

I reminded myself that that's like rule number one of best friend code. Siblings are completely and utterly off limits.

But as I thought about Kenzie's alert eyes, shining blond hair that smelled of apples and flowers, and the way her lips curl up into a half-smile when she talked about anything she's passionate about, I wondered if it was too late.

I grabbed my phone and shot her a text.

Great. I'll meet you there at one ;)

CHAPTER 7

I stared at Gavin's text in front of me.

Great. I'll meet you there at one ;)

A sudden warmth radiated throughout my core. I'd expected him to reschedule for tomorrow, not agree to volunteering at the new nursing home my mother just opened while cramming in study sessions. And he sent one of those winky faces back to me.

His grade must be seriously bad.

I stepped in front of the dresser mirror and frowned at my reflection. I'd stayed up all night reading, well, rereading for the fourth time, *Emma* by Jane Austen, so there were two dark bags cupping my eyes. Strands of blond hair had fallen from a braid at the crown of my head because I hadn't even touched it up after climbing out of bed this morning.

And then there was my outfit. *Ugh*. I could barely

stand to look at the pair of baggy, old, gray sweatpants that frayed at the bottom and a sweatshirt that'd seen better days with the words *Be-you-tiful* on the front.

Um, yeah. Decidedly not beautiful this morning.

"Leaving in fifteen minutes, Kenz!" Mom yelled from downstairs, her voice echoing through the hallway and then bouncing into my room.

"Got it!" I glanced at the time. 12:30.

I tore through my closet and then through my dresser, hoping to find something that said casual, yet cute. After digging through, cringe, the hamper, I settled on a pair of leggings with a dark green sweater. I tossed on a pair of black flats and then darted to my bathroom. In a mad rush, I re-braided the locks of hair and pinned them behind my ears, put on a coat of mascara, pinched my cheeks for color, and then dabbed on my favorite strawberry lip-gloss.

"You coming?" Mom yelled.

I gave myself a final glance in the mirror and sighed, satisfied at the girl who looked back. "Be right down, Ma!"

I grabbed my book bag and bounded down the stairs, two steps at a time.

When I got to the bottom, Mom's eyes glanced from the tip of my head to my flats. She appraised me and pressed her lips together. "You sure look cute for a day of work." She raised an eyebrow.

I shrugged. "Thanks," I muttered, unsure of how she expected me to answer.

"I thought I'd put you on bathroom duty?"

I stopped dead in my tracks. "What?"

Mom flicked her wrist at me. "Just kidding." She laughed, obviously finding herself amusing. "We ordered just over two thousand books for the reading room, so I thought you wouldn't mind getting them shelved."

I grinned. "That's actually perfect."

And even more perfect to have Gavin helping me.

* * *

We pulled up to Cedar Oaks Retirement Center to see large block letters posted on a banner out front.

Now Accepting Residents.
Grand Opening—November 4

I glanced at my mom and smiled, so proud that she'd been the one to make this happen.

Before I was born, Mom managed the nursing home across town. She decided to leave that job and become a stay-at-home mom to me and Cory. We were always lucky because my dad, who was an accountant, earned enough money that Mom didn't have to go back to work. Still, over the years, she picked up part-time nursing jobs around town and loved every minute of it. She even did a few part-time stints as a barista at Cafe Prose, a saleswoman at a local boutique, and a designer at the local florist. But she always missed her role at the retirement home. Especially in organizing the placement of elderly whose families had basically abandoned them.

Because Cedar Oaks only had two homes for the elderly, both of which had their own administrators, Mom decided to take matters in her own hands. A year after Dad died, she applied for a nursing position with the local hospital where she picked up every overtime, holiday shift. Over the past two years, she'd put as much money as she could into savings. With that money, even more of what Dad left her, and a lot of help from a few investors, Mom took a gamble and bought an old apartment complex and decided to make her dreams come true. And her dream would be opening early next month.

I always wished to be as brave as Mom.

"Congrats, Ma," I whispered, gesturing toward the refurbed building.

She wrapped an arm around me and squeezed. "Thank you for all your help, Kenzie." She leaned over and kissed me atop my head.

"I wouldn't *not* help, Mom." I wriggled my nose. "Cory on the other hand?"

Mom grunted. "He's hanging out with his girlfriend over helping me, so ..." she teased. She made the come-here motion with her hand. "Let me show you where you'll be working today."

We walked through the entryway foyer, with a reception desk situated in the right-hand corner, and then she led me to a large room off the grand entrance.

"There are the books." She pointed to at least a dozen large boxes with books of all sorts spilling over—romances, Westerns, science fiction, classics, and more.

I picked up a copy of *Metamorphosis*. "How do you expect me to sort these when all I want to do is read?"

Mom laughed. "You'll figure it out." She turned. "I need to get a few things situated with the contractor, so have fun!"

"Oh, I will." I smirked and then glanced at my phone —12:57—suddenly feeling my chest tighten. In a matter of minutes Gavin would be here. I looked at my reflection in one of the glass cabinets, refreshed my lip-gloss, and then got to work, trying as best I could to push the nerves aside.

Breathe.

I emptied the first box of romance books. "Where did Mom get these?" I muttered. Underneath a stack of sweet, chaste covers were a dozen or so Harlequin romance novels with half-naked men adorning the cover in compromising positions. I grabbed one from the top and just as I looked down at the title I heard a throat clear behind me. "What you up to?" a voice asked.

I turned around slowly.

Act casual, Kenz. Don't be a spaz. That should have been my mantra by now.

"Hey, Gavin." I held up the book I'd just grabbed from the stack. "Just checking out this book." I glanced at the cover and felt my face flame red as Gavin took it from my hands. This cover photo depicted one of those scantily clad men ripping back the bodice of a large-busted woman.

"I didn't realize this was your thing, Kenzie."

I snatched the book from Gavin's hands and tossed it

back in the box. "I was ... um ..." I looked to the floor. "Just starting to sort and stuff."

Gavin moved to the romance box and held up another book. "I think my mom reads these." He leafed through the book and then set it down. "So what's the plan?" He searched a reaction from me.

I shrugged like an idiot. *Get yourself together. You've known Gavin forever.* As if that small pep-talk to myself helped, I spoke. "Well, how about we sort for two hours and then study?"

Gavin smiled the crooked smile I'd grown to adore. "Sounds like a plan."

"Let's start with romance."

I felt my heart beat in my throat as Gavin's deep blue eyes, eyes as blue as the sky, met mine. He sent me a half smile. "Let's start there."

And as much as I knew I shouldn't read into his response, part of me hoped the beginning of our own love story was starting too.

CHAPTER 8

If you counted the number of books I'd held in my hands over the past eighteen years, it wouldn't even come close to the number of books I'd touched over the past two hours.

"One more box to go," Kenzie chirped. She raised an eyebrow and her green eyes peered at me behind thick eyelashes.

She is beautiful.

We sorted through the box of historical fiction—yawn—and then sat at the small round table in the center of the retirement home's reading room. I looked at our handiwork of organized books lining a floor-to-ceiling bookshelf and then glanced down the hallway. "Your mom did an awesome job with this place."

Kenzie's lips curled up at the ends. "She sure did." I could tell she was proud of Mrs. Fair, and the smile on her face, coupled with the pride she held for her mother made Kenzie even more attractive.

I locked eyes with her. "Your dad would be so proud of her, Kenz."

Kenzie ran her hand across her notebook and when she looked up, tears glistened under the overhead lights. She brushed one away with the back of her hand. "He would."

I looked away and pulled out my copy of the play, giving Kenzie a moment to compose herself. When I peered back up at her though, she was staring at me.

"What is it?"

Kenzie pushed a piece of blond hair from her face and spoke cautiously. "I never thanked you for being here."

I wrinkled my face. She was doing *me* the favor. "What do you mean? I should be thanking you."

Kenzie sighed. "Not here, *here*. I mean here for us. For me. Mom. Cory." She paused. "After Dad died."

I studied her face and the way her bottom lip trembled. "Really, Kenzie. You know I'd do anything for you." I cleared my throat. "For you all."

As I said the words aloud, I realized I meant them more than I'd ever meant them before.

She smiled and sniffed back the last tear. "Well, thank you, Gavin."

"You're welcome." I gestured toward the play. "Now I believe we have some Shakespeareing to do."

Kenzie opened her notebook and flipped through page after page of notes. I glanced at the top of the first page and spoke. "Are all of those notes on Act 3?"

"Yeah." She looked at me and pushed her chin to the

air. "And how many pages of notes do you have, pray tell?"

I liked the way she'd just used a Shakespearean word. "I'll have thine know, I took a grand total of one page of noteths." As soon as the sentence escaped my mouth, in a goofy lofty tone, no less, I wanted to take it back.

Kenzie leaned her head back and laughed—a genuine belly laugh like the ones she would make when I'd find her while playing hide-and-seek as kids.

"Hey!" I protested in jest. "I tried."

Kenzie pulled my notebook to her side of the table and then scribbled down two words. She pointed to the first one.

"Thee," I said. "And thou."

Kenzie nodded. "So thee and thou both mean you." She wrote down one more word.

"Thine," I pronounced.

"Thine is possessive, so it's like using *your*."

I leaned back in my chair. "How do you just know this stuff?"

"I read a lot." Kenzie shrugged. "And I just love the Bard."

"The what?"

She flicked a hand at me. "Shakespeare. He was also called the ..." Kenzie cut herself off.

"He was also called what?"

Kenzie frowned. "You don't want to hear me nerd out."

I leaned toward her and met her eyes so she knew I was serious. "But I do. I like when you *nerd out*." I weighed whether or not to say what was on my mind, but decided to go for it. "I think it's cute."

On that last word, I swore Kenzie's cheeks flushed pink. She bit the side of her lip, and then spoke. "The Bard was another title for Shakespeare. The meaning of the word bard is poet, and Shakespeare was arguably the most talented poet to have ever lived."

"The Bard." I rolled the title over my tongue. "I kind of like it."

Kenzie opened her copy of *A Midsummer Night's Dream*. "Well, I'm glad you do, because we have some of his words to study."

"Touché," I said, hoping I at least used that word correctly.

The next two hours flew by, and before I knew it, Kenzie had created a practice quiz for me to take.

She ran a purple pen down the margin as her eyes scanned my responses. She set the pen down, leaned back in her chair, and smiled. "Perfect score!"

"I don't get why Lysander didn't just confess his love?" I started. "If he did that in the first place, then they wouldn't be in the predicament to begin with."

Kenzie smiled shyly and chewed on her lip. "It seems you're getting Shakespeare more than you let on. Are you sure you have a D?"

I laughed. If only she knew how inept I was in English. "Oh, I'm very sure."

"Well, you seem to be understanding the play much better."

I put down my pen and locked eyes with her. "I think it's my pretty tutor."

I'm not sure why I said those words ... they just spilled out. And right after I said them, it was like all the air was sucked out of the room at once.

We sat in silence as Kenzie played with the sleeve of her sweater. "So I ... uh ... I think we're good then." She shut her notebook and shoved it into her bag. Her eyes darted to me and then to the ground. "Anything else?"

I rubbed a hand to my neck, wishing I could get a better read on her. I cleared my throat. "So, there's this party tonight at Emma Good's ..." I hesitated, gauging her response

"Okay?" she prompted, her eyes settling back on me.

Whatever awkwardness just enveloped the room vanished. I stood, zippered up my bag, and tossed it over my shoulder. "Do you wanna go?"

Kenzie chewed at her lip. "Well ... I'm not exactly the party type."

I stepped closer to her. "Wanna know a secret?" I leaned down, so my lips were just inches from her ear. I inhaled the air as a blend of apple and strawberry filled my nose. "I'm not either."

Kenzie rolled her eyes. "For the past two years all you and Cory do on the weekend is go to parties. Flirt with girls. Make out with Claire ..." Kenzie's voice trailed off at the end as she shook her head. "I'm sorry."

I laughed. "If that's what you think, then you're misinformed." I raised a finger in the air. "I'll have you know two things. One—Claire and I are done." That was something that, for some reason, I wanted to make clear to Kenzie. I raised another finger. "And two—my idea of partying is finding the closest television in whoever's house I'm in, and playing Soccer Xtreme."

Kenzie narrowed her eyes. "Really?" She wasn't buying it.

I tilted my head. "I'll prove it."

"And how will you do that?" Her tone was different ... almost taunting. *Is Kenzie flirting with me?*

"Come to the party and see for yourself." I outstretched my arm and brushed Kenzie's hand with my fingertips.

She gasped and then pulled her hand away, moving it to her lap. Her eyes trailed behind and settled on her lap too.

I stepped toward the door. "Guess you'll never know then."

Just as I reached for the knob, Kenzie spoke. "Wait." I pivoted around to see her eyes focused on mine.

She smirked. "I'll go."

I smiled inside. "It's a date." I paused. "I mean, not a date. It's a ..." Gosh, now I was the one rambling. "How about I pick you up around eight?"

CHAPTER 9

"It's totally official." Veda handed me my vanilla latte she'd just grabbed from the coffee bar and then shimmied her shoulders. "Gavin Mitchell has a thing for his best friend's sister," she sing-songed.

"Shh!" I leaned forward and smacked her on the arm. "He does not."

Veda raised her eyebrows up and down, up and down. "I think tonight is the perfect time to tell him how you feel … how you've felt for a while."

I chewed the inside of my cheek, careful not to get too excited. "I'm not sure about that."

"I've tried to get you to go to parties with me for the last year and a half. All it took was Gavin asking you." Veda pursed her lips and her bangles jangled as she flicked her hand at me. "I see how I rank."

I put out a hand. "Come on, Veda."

She giggled. "You know it's totally fine. This is what

you've wanted for years!" Veda held her fists close to her chest and squealed.

I pulled my lips to the side. "It's not a date or anything."

"Yes, but here's the big question ..." She groaned.

"Yeah?"

"What does your brother think?"

"What do you mean?"

"I mean." Veda leaned in closer. "Does he know Gavin asked you to the party?"

I rolled my eyes. "I don't need to be asked to show up at Emma Good's party. She invites the entire school."

Veda looked at me over her mug. "True, but won't your brother think it's odd you show up with Gavin?"

I shrugged. "I don't know. We're just friends." I traced the edge of my lid. "He simply mentioned the party after our tutoring session, I said I might go, and he happened to offer me a ride."

Veda lifted an eyebrow. "If you say so."

"What? Nothing is going to happen anyway, so there's nothing for Cory to know."

Veda leaned back in her chair and rolled her eyes. "Okay, Kenz."

"Well ..." I paused and leaned forward. "There was this part when he called me pretty," I whispered.

Veda's eyes widened and she dramatically slapped me on the arm. "And you're just mentioning this now ... because?"

I scrunched my face. "Suspense?"

"Well, then this whole librarian look you have going

for you." She looked me over, from my most comfortable pair of jeans to my sensible, weather-appropriate sweater. "Although super cute, this." She waved her pointer finger up and down. "Is not what I'd call party-worthy."

"Hey!" I protested. I brushed a hand down my sweater, smoothing out the wrinkles. "I resent that."

"Let me do a make-over on you."

I played with my fraying sleeves. "I'll throw on something cuter, I promise."

Veda pulled her lips to the side.

"What?" I asked, sensing there was more.

"Can I just put a little makeup on you?"

Veda knew that my makeup routine, which took me a whopping sixty seconds, consisted of throwing in my contacts, brushing on some mascara, dabbing on lip-gloss, and pinching my cheeks for color. I looked up at my best friend who gave me puppy-dog eyes, pouted her lips, and batted her eyelashes. "Please? I'll make you look totally kissable."

My stomach flipped at the sound of her last word. *Kissable.*

She just wanted to help, and it wouldn't hurt to spruce up my look for Gavin Mitchell. And if I got my first kiss out of it with the boy of my dreams, then even better.

"Fine," I relented.

* * *

"Be home by eleven!" Mom shouted from her office as

I stepped on the front porch. I loved that I had a curfew of eleven, while Cory—who was only a year and a half older than me—never got one. Oh, the joys of being the younger sister.

"Okay, Mom," I shouted, in no mood to argue the double standard of curfew and gender.

I shut the door and then pulled my jacket close to my body, wrapping it around the black and purple dress Veda let me borrow for the night. I tugged at the dress's bottom hem so the material fell four inches or so above my knees.

"I can't believe Veda talked me into this." I muttered.

Veda had left about thirty minutes ago, after what she claimed was "a beauty emergency". I turned to look at her handiwork in the windows flanking the front door and smiled. Veda had pulled my hair in a low messy bun—a look I'd been unsuccessful at attempting on my own for the past year. She'd elevated my less-is-more look by adding some eyeshadow that glittered slightly under the right light, eyeliner that emphasized my eyes, and a berry-colored lipstick that made my lips look plump and, dare I say, kissable.

I hated to admit it, but Veda was totally right. Although there was nothing wrong with my casual, yet slightly bookish look, a dab of makeup and different hairstyle went a long way.

I glanced at my phone. 8:07.

Where is Gavin?

As if he read my thought, his red Jeep turned the corner of my street and then pulled into the driveway.

My heart beat a little faster as I moved forward on the porch, awkwardly holding my hand over my eyes to shield the bright headlights washing over the house. I leaned heavily on the railing, holding myself up, careful not to stumble in the four-inch platforms Veda suggested I wear. Well, she didn't suggest. It was more of a demand.

One wrong move, and you're so going down.

Suddenly, a car door slammed in front of me, and I heard footsteps getting closer and closer. "Do you need help?" Gavin asked. Although I couldn't see his face due to the blinding headlights, I could practically hear the smirk in his voice. *Ugh.* I could only imagine the look of amusement on his face as I walked down the stairs like a toddler taking its first steps.

I'm sure this is a great look.

As my shoe landed on the sidewalk, I felt my ankle give way atop the platforms. "Oh, shoot!" I muttered, my body lurching forward. I expected to fall onto the solid ground below, but two hands grabbed the space just behind my elbows as I crashed into something hard.

It wasn't just something. My jaw dropped as I felt Gavin's chest muscles tighten under my face.

"Are you alright?" Gavin asked. His arms felt strong and warm as they cupped my arms.

"I am such a spaz," I muttered.

Gavin propped me up and looked me in my eyes. A facial expression I couldn't quite read crossed his face. In fact, it was the same, confusing expression he made that first night I'd tutored him.

"No problem." His voice came out a whisper.

Suddenly I was aware—no, more than aware—of the two warm hands that still gently held my arms.

Gavin rubbed a hand up and down my sleeve. "I happen to think that 'spaz' is an adorable quality." My head snapped up and I looked up at him. His blue eyes, eyes alert and gorgeous, stared into mine. I couldn't look away. Gavin took a hand from my arm and brushed a piece of hair from my cheek. After his fingers tucked the blond strands behind my ear, he didn't pull them away; they rested on the sensitive space just below my ear. A sudden warmth grew beneath his fingers and spread through my face. And as much as I didn't want to tear my eyes from his, this was so foreign ... so new ... to me. Unsure of what to do, of the feelings that suddenly overwhelmed me, I looked to my shoes.

"You're just saying that because you're my brother's best friend," I murmured.

Gavin cupped my chin in his hand and tilted my head up so my eyes couldn't *not* meet his. He swallowed and stepped toward me. "Actually ..." He hesitated. "I shouldn't say that *because* I'm your brother's best friend."

A million thoughts rushed through my head at once. First, Gavin smelled divine—vanilla, pine, and a faint note of fresh soap. Second, I was pretty sure Gavin Mitchell, my brother's best friend since forever, my crush since practically forever, was about to kiss me. And third, I had no idea what I was doing.

Gavin pulled me toward him and moved forward, closing the gap between us.

What is happening? What is happening? What is happening?

In what felt like a natural movement, I tilted my head in the air, lips leading the way. Gavin leaned toward me, but just as our faces were mere inches from each other, he stepped away.

"I'm sorry, Kenzie." Gavin threw a hand to his head and groaned. "Cory would kill me." He pushed some pebbles around with his toe and leaned an arm against the white stair rail.

My face became hot, and I could have died of embarrassment right then and there. I stumbled backward. "I need to go," I muttered. I saw Gavin reach an arm toward me, but before he could catch me, I'd bounded up the stairs, ignoring the pain in my feet, and ran into the house.

"Wait! Kenzie!" he shouted.

Just before I slammed the door in his face, his voice called through the door. "You look really pretty tonight."

I leaned my head on the door and put a hand to my head.

What just happened?

CHAPTER 10

I got to Emma's house as the sound of music blasted out the front door. A group of seniors from my chemistry class stumbled onto the porch. To the right, a couple was cuddling on a porch swing. When I stepped inside the large Victorian home, complete with its turreted rooms and antiquated woodwork, it looked like any other Saturday night get-together in Cedar Oaks.

I was beginning to think staying home, curled up on the couch, reading or relaxing or whatever Mackenzie has done throughout high school on the weekends was a much better option than being here.

Mackenzie. I pushed her name from my head. But for some reason these past few days, that was impossible.

"Hey, man!" Cory greeted me in the entryway and slapped my hand. "Where have you been?" He eyed me suspiciously.

"Um ..." I swallowed and licked my lips, prepping myself for the lie. "Just had some studying to do."

Mark Watson, Cedar Oaks' starting goalie, jumped in. "Cory's hot little sis is helping you, right?"

"Hey!" Cory jerked his arm backward, giving Mark a solid blow to the ribs with his elbow.

"Ugh,'" Mark groaned. He leaned over and put two hands to the spot Cory's elbow met a second ago. "What was that for?"

Cory narrowed his eyes. "I think you know."

I shuddered. That wasn't the first time Cory hit someone who talked about his sister.

Cory can't know how much I thought about kissing Kenzie in his front yard just ten minutes ago.

Cory bumped my shoulder with the bottom of his cup. "You should be eligible for playoffs, right?"

I played with the edge of my jacket. "Yep. After Monday's quiz, I should be set."

"Game's set up in the back room. I'm gonna grab a drink then will be there." Cory slapped the back of his hand to my shoulder. "Need one?"

I nodded. "A Mountain Dew would be great. I could use the caffeine."

Cory moved to the kitchen, and just before he walked through the door, Emma found him and threw two arms around his neck. "I've been looking for you, Core," she purred. I knew he wouldn't be joining me for Soccer Xtreme anytime soon, so I grabbed my own soda from the cooler in the dining room and then made my way to the sunroom.

I plopped myself on the oversized leather sofa, took a sip of soda, and then grabbed the controller from the coffee table. Just as my avatar got into starting position, I felt two arms snake around my neck.

"Hey, handsome." I looked down at the hands below my chin and cringed as soon as I spied the long, pink fingernails. Claire.

I set down the controller and unlatched Claire's hands.

"Eck!" she huffed. The couch shifted under me as she took the spot directly to my right.

I rolled my eyes. "This is a huge couch, you know?" I gestured to the other end a good three feet away.

"What's your problem?"

My problem was that I was over superficial girls like Claire. Sure, she was absolutely gorgeous, but gorgeous didn't interest me anymore. I wanted to be with someone like ...

"Earth to Gavee-poo!" Claire waved a skinny arm in front of my face.

I ignored her and picked up the game controller again. Claire's cool hand ran across my neck and I slunk away.

"Come on." She turned up her nose. "What's going on?"

I snapped my head toward her. "What is going on is I'm tired of you trying to do"—I pointed to her and then to me and then back and forth again—"whatever this is you're trying to do." I clenched my jaw. "It's not going to work, Claire."

Claire flicked a few strands of brown hair behind her back and spoke. "Is it just me, or ..." Her voice trailed off and she appraised me narrowly. "I just want to know what's going on in that head of yours?"

I narrowed my eyes at her. "You're saying that as if you'd have a reason to care. We've been broken up for a month, Claire. Done. Over."

Claire became uncharacteristically quiet, and I felt her eyes burning into the side of my face. "You've met someone." Her words were certain.

Was it that obvious?

I refused to respond.

Claire's weight lifted from the space next to me. "Whatever, Gavin," she spat.

I sighed in relief as she left the room, the clacking of her heels becoming softer and softer as she moved down the hallway.

"Hey, man!" Noah grabbed the remote next to me while Veda took the spot next to him on the loveseat to my left. "Thought you were bringing Cory's little sister."

I noticed Veda give her boyfriend the eyes.

Noah laughed. "Whoops. I wasn't supposed to know about that, huh?"

"It's not like it was some big secret. I was just gonna bring her along."

Veda stepped in front of the television; my cue to stop playing the game. "Kenzie called me."

I swallowed hard. "She did?"

Veda put a bracelet-covered wrist on her hip and pursed her lips. "Come on, Gavin. You've had to have known she's had a crush on you, like, forever now." She crossed her arms over her chest. "How could you toy with her like that?"

I shook my head. "I didn't mean ..."

And I'd just led her on and then left her.

"What an idiot ..." I muttered. I dropped the remote. "I need to talk to her. Explain ..." I trailed off.

Noah nudged my shoulder. "Well, now's your chance, bro."

Veda held up her phone so I could read the message that popped up.

Kenz: Just got to Emma's. Where r u?

My eyes got wide. "She's here?"

Veda nodded. "She needed to see me."

I darted up from the couch. "I need to talk to her first."

Veda smirked. "I think that's a great idea."

I pushed my way through the crowded house, nudging people out of the way with my elbows.

"Where are you off to?" Claire asked.

I ignored her snark, rushing past her, and just as my hand reached the doorknob, the oak door in front of me swung open.

I stopped in my tracks at the sight of Kenzie. Her hair no longer was pulled up, but locks of blond hair just brushing her shoulders glistened in the light—light that made her eyes appear a deep emerald green.

"Can we talk for a second?" I asked, shutting the door behind me.

Kenzie took a step back onto the porch. She bit her lip. "I think you made yourself clear earlier."

"Look. I'm sorry about —."

"No need to apologize." Kenzie put her hand to my chest and an electric buzz vibrated under her touch and spread through my core, just like it'd done earlier tonight.

As if Kenzie felt it too, she retracted her hand and shoved it into her jacket pocket, pulling her coat tighter around her.

"I'm not sure what happened at your house ... it's just." I paused.

Kenzie smiled ever so slightly, and I watched as her chest rose and fell in faster bursts.

"What I said about your brother ..." I sighed. "He would hate me."

Kenzie rolled her eyes. "I'm not a little girl anymore. Ever since Dad—." She cleared her throat. "Ever since then, Cory's treated me like a baby. I'm practically an adult."

I moved closer to her. "Have you told Cory that?"

Kenzie shrugged. "Not exactly."

I weighed whether or not to say what was on my mind, but realized I couldn't keep it in any longer. "I think there could be something ... here." I stepped closer to Kenzie, inhaled the strawberry scent surrounding her, and swallowed. "Between us."

Kenzie tucked a loose piece of hair behind her ear. Her voice came out a whisper. "I do too."

I reached out a hand and tugged on the sleeve of her jacket, pulling her toward me. "And I never wanted to admit it, but I think I might have had feelings for you for a while."

Mackenzie scrunched her face, and the way her nose scrunched to the side made her look adorable and cute and completely kissable.

"Really?" she asked.

"Yes." I smiled, happy to finally say it out loud. "And the past few days just confirmed it." Cory or not, I knew for a fact my feelings for Mackenzie Fair were real, and the words I said were true.

Kenzie just stared back at me ... speechless. The same piece of hair that struggled to remain behind her ear came loose again.

I brushed it from her face and let my hand rest on her neck and the hollow space just above her collarbone I so desperately wanted to kiss. I swallowed. "Now what do you think we should do about it?"

Kenzie answered by stepping forward. I moved my other hand to her back and pulled her toward me. Her eyes met mine as I leaned in, inching closer and closer to her face. To her lips.

When our faces were a mere inch from meeting, Kenzie spoke. "I've ..." She looked to my lips and then back to my eyes and sighed.

What did I do?

Kenzie whispered, "I've never kissed anyone before."

I hesitated and then moved my hand to just under her chin. I gently lifted her face toward me and then drew my hand away. "It's okay." I stepped back from her and smiled. "No need to rush anything."

When her eyes met mine though, I felt a heat spread across my chest. Her look was so intense, so ... perfect.

She parted her lips to speak and her voice came out a whisper. "But I never said I didn't want to right now."

And that was all the confirmation I needed. I closed the space between us and wrapped one hand behind her neck. Her skin was soft under my touch. She leaned forward, her eyes slipping from my eyes and then settling on my lips. I closed the gap and our lips touched. Kenzie's lips were soft and warm and tasted like strawberries, as good as I imagined. I pulled away and met her eyes, wondering if this was okay.

A smile and slight nod of Kenzie's head told me it was.

"I've wanted to do that for a while," I admitted.

Kenzie smiled. "And I've wanted you to," she whispered.

I cupped her chin and tilted it toward me. But this time, as our lips just brushed, light as feathers, the clicking of the front door sounded.

Kenzie and I jumped apart

"Waitin' for you, man," Cory said, bounding onto the porch. I spun around, and his eyes moved from me and settled on his sister.

"I see you've decided to come out of your hole tonight," he teased.

I rubbed the back of my neck and then pointed to a blushing Kenzie. "Uh ... Kenz had to drop off some notes for English."

I inwardly cringed. *Please don't notice there are no notes in sight.*

"Yeah." Kenzie clenched her jaw as I sent her what-was-I-supposed-to-say eyes.

Cory shrugged. "Nerds."

I followed Cory inside, leaving Kenzie alone in the cold fall air.

What had I gotten myself into?

But I knew the answer.

I have it bad for my best friend's sister.

CHAPTER 11

I didn't turn back into the little cinder girl, arriving home just shy of my curfew. I bounded up the stairs, two at a time, and floated into my bedroom.

Not literally floated, obviously. But I definitely felt lighter than air as the memory of my first kissed played and then replayed in my head.

Gavin Mitchell kissed me.

Saying it in my head just didn't make it feel real enough. "Gavin Mitchell kissed me," I said aloud. Tonight, my dreams literally came true. I twisted my hair up into a messy bun and then let go, watching the curls fall to my shoulders. I used the tips of my fingers to add volume to the roots and then puckered my lips. "Not too bad, Veda," I muttered. Her makeover from hours ago held its own.

I giggled to myself and then brushed the hair down. I

wasn't the only one practically jumping out of my skin in excitement. After I'd relayed the events ... mainly the kiss ... of the evening to Veda, she'd literally jumped up and down, her jewelry clinking and clanking with each bounce.

My phone vibrated in my purse, jarring me from my thoughts. I rummaged through it and just about fainted when Gavin's name lit up on the screen.

Gavin: *Hope your first kiss didn't disappoint.* ;)

I tapped my fingers on the screen, weighing what to answer back. I could say *it was great*. But that didn't even come close to describing it. And I didn't want to over-describe it by saying *it was the most magnificent experience I've ever had and it felt like a million butterflies took flight in my stomach as soon as your lips met mine.* Although true, that would be a bit much, and the last thing I'd want to do is scare off the guy I've had a thing for for over three years.

I touched two fingers to my lips, thinking back to the kiss once more, and how I literally felt a tingle start in my lips and spread the entire way to my toes when Gavin kissed me. "He kissed me!" I pulled my phone toward my chest and tapped out a response.

Kenzie: *It was perfect.*

Short and sweet and true in every way. I leaned back on my bed and sighed. And then the reality of what just happened hit me. Yes, Gavin Mitchell kissed me. Ahmaze-ing. But more problematically—my brother's best friend just kissed me. Not so amazing.

But wouldn't Cory be happy to know my first kiss was with his best friend, someone he'd known practically his entire life, rather than with a jerk like ... like ... Michael Sands?

Ick.

My phone vibrated against my side.

Gavin: *Was thinking maybe we could do it again?*

The three bubbles popped up under that message, indicating he was typing more.

Gavin: *I think I need a little more help with act 3. ;)*

I flipped over on my belly, knees bent, with the bottoms of my feet to the ceiling, and tapped back a response.

Kenzie: *It's a date. ;)*

I held my breath and hit send.
I smiled as soon as his response reached my phone.

Gavin: *A date, indeed.*

* * *

After another morning of sorting books at the new retirement center, I headed home to meet Gavin for our study session. I knew Mom would be spending her afternoon at the home, and even better—Cory's Sunday gym routine started at one, so I told Gavin to meet me at one-thirty.

When I opened the front door to see him standing on the other side, I couldn't stop the smile from spreading across my face. He looked cuter than ever in a pair of jeans, long-sleeved gray t-shirt, and a pair of Converse.

"Hey." Gavin leaned forward and pecked me on the cheek. I inhaled his clove and pine cologne and pinched the side of my wrist to make sure this was actually happening.

Ouch. It was.

"Hi!" I finally said, taking a step backward as Gavin moved inside.

Gavin reached a hand down and scratched Muffin behind her ears. "Hey, little girl!"

This time I took a step back, giving him room for the greeting. I didn't want any chance of accidentally giving him a concussion like I'd almost done a few days ago.

And then it hit me ... a few days ago. Just a few days ago I'd daydreamed about kissing Gavin Mitchell, and now it was my reality. How did this happen so fast?

Gavin ran his hand down the backpack strap on his shoulder and then slung the bag to the ground. "So, I need to confess." I frowned, imagining he was about to tell me this was some mistake.

But Gavin smiled and continued. "The main reason I set up another study session was to see you." Gavin grabbed my hand and rubbed the soft spot between my thumb and index finger. I practically melted.

"But." He dropped my hand, bent over, and grabbed his copy of *Midsummer*. "But I actually do need a little more help before tomorrow's quiz."

I tilted my head to the side and peered at him over my glasses. "Are you using me for my brains, Mr. Mitchell?" I teased, in disbelief of how easily the flirtation slipped out.

Gavin stepped toward me. "Maybe." He winked and then tapped the side of my frames. "Have I ever told you how cute glasses look on you?"

I chewed the cherry Chapstick off my bottom lip. "You've never told me, actually." I felt the blood rush to my face. Why did all of his compliments do that to me?

Although I'd loved my dolled-up look from last night's party, I was in no mood to put that much effort into my look this afternoon. If Gavin wanted to see me, he was going to see the real glasses-wearing, book-reading, library-loving Mackenzie Fair. But in all honesty, he'd known who I was for years, so there was no need to be anyone else.

"Well, we read through the entire act yesterday, and I'm pretty sure you've got it." I bit my lip. "So ... I thought maybe we could watch the movie."

"For supplemental help," Gavin added with an assured nod.

I swallowed hard, quite aware of what happens in dark basements.

"Come on." We moved down the stairs and I flicked on the light. Just as we got situated on the sofa, Gavin turned to me.

"So how long, Kenz?"

I wrinkled my nose. "How long what?"

Gavin scooted closer and grabbed my hand. He traced the palm of my hand with his fingertip. "How long have you had a crush on me? Veda said ..." His voice trailed off.

My head grew hot. "I'm gonna hurt her," I muttered.

Gavin tossed his head back and laughed. "For real though. How long?"

I inhaled and slowly released my breath. "Since eighth grade. Right after ..." I shrugged. "You know."

Gavin smiled a sad smile. "Yeah. I know."

He squeezed my hand as I willed away the tears that sprang to my eyes any time my father's death came up. "And what about you? When did you start crushing on me?"

"Honestly?" Gavin ran a hand through his hair, one of his favorite gestures I never tired of. I watched his bicep muscle tense under his t-shirt. He swallowed. "Since then too."

Wait. What?

My jaw dropped. "Really?"

Gavin nodded. "Well ... I think I tried to tell myself I couldn't have feelings for you because of Cory. Because after that happened with your dad, you needed me, but in a different way. And as much as I tried to convince myself I saw you as Cory's little sister, it was these past few days"—he paused and ran a finger up my arm—"spending time together, that I realized I'd been lying to myself." He scooted closer to me. "I haven't seen you as Cory's little sister in a very long time."

I stared into his blue eyes. "You haven't?"

Gavin shook his head from side to side. "You're smart and beautiful, Kenzie, and I've fallen for you." He gestured to me and then back at himself. "Whatever this is ... I want it to work out."

I felt multiple emotions flood over me at once. Relief that he felt the way I did. Excitement for whatever this was. And guilt for keeping it a secret. I pulled away. "Then we need to tell Cory."

Gavin nodded. "Yeah, but not before playoffs."

I nodded. "Right after then."

"Yes." He let go of my hand. "Well, we only have about an hour, so we should get started?"

I stood up and found the movie in the cabinet and then popped it in the archaic DVD player. I skipped to Act 3 and then moved to the couch.

Gavin grabbed my wrist and pulled me down so I sunk into the sofa next to him, our legs touching. He wrapped an arm around my shoulder and turned toward me. "How do you expect me to watch this when I have the most gorgeous girl in the world sitting next to me?"

I quirked an eyebrow. "You have two options."

"Oh, yeah?"

I nodded and pointed to the screen where Queen

Titania lay in her nest. "You put me out of your mind the best you can and focus on this movie, and this movie alone."

"Or?" He raised an eyebrow and turned his body toward me, obviously sensing the second option.

My heart thrummed in my chest at the prospect of kissing Gavin again. He cupped my chin in his hand and gently pulled my face forward. This time, I didn't just sit there and let the kiss happen. I moved toward him and wrapped my hand around the back of his neck, his hair tickling my fingers. Gavin's eyes moved from mine and then stared at my lips. In what felt like slow motion, he tilted his head and moved toward me. His lips just brushed mine when the doorbell rang.

Gavin jolted backward with a mischievous smile on his face. I watched as his chest heaved up and down.

"It's just the doorbell." I bumped his shoulder with mine.

He cleared his throat. "Darn doorbell," he said, his voice low and smooth.

The doorbell rang again, this time three dings in a row. I looked toward the stairs. "I should get that."

I ran up the stairs, and as I opened the front door, Veda rushed past me, bringing with her the cold autumn air.

"Gavin's here," I said through my teeth, hoping she'd catch my tone.

Veda fiddled with her fingers—a nervous maneuver my best friend was way too confident to use. She bit at the side of her lip. "You and Gavin have a little problem."

She pushed her phone to my face.

I looked at the picture on her screen and my mouth fell to the floor. "This was from last night." I tried to wrap my mind around it. "But ... how?" I pulled the phone closer to my face and felt my stomach drop.

Me. Gavin. Last night. On the porch.

Someone had taken a picture of my first kiss.

CHAPTER 12

I stared at the photograph on Veda's phone and punched the air. "Michael Sands." I clenched and unclenched my jaw. What a jerk.

Veda put the phone in her back pocket. "And there's more."

Kenzie stepped forward. "More than the picture?"

Veda sighed and a pained expression crossed her face, as if it literally hurt her to be the one delivering whatever message she had to relay. "Michael told Noah that if he doesn't play striker in Wednesday's game, then he'll send the picture to Cory." She put a hand to her head. "And to the rest of the team for that matter."

"Oh my goodness," Kenzie said, mimicking my own disbelief.

Veda hugged Kenzie. "I need to meet my mom for lunch, but I'll call later."

Kenzie nodded slowly. "Thanks, Veda,"

As Veda made her way down the sidewalk, I felt a

vibration in my back pocket. I pulled out my phone to see a new text with the photo in question attached ... from Michael, jerk face, Sands.

> Michael: *Throw Fretz's quiz or this gets sent to everyone.*

"He wants me to fail the quiz." I clenched and unclenched my fists. "That's why he was egging you on the other day, Kenzie. He wanted to distract you from tutoring me—thinking he was finally getting his chance to play." I hit the side of my fist into the doorframe. "To take my position on the field."

Kenzie furrowed her eyebrows. "So what if he does send Cory the picture?" She stood up straighter and stuck out her chest, an act of confidence that took my breath away. "Can't he just get over it?" Kenzie stepped closer to me and grabbed my hand. "You're his best friend, not some unknown jerk who's just using me."

I leaned my head against the door. "Cory would kill me. His head would never be in the game, and if I'm not playing and Cory's not playing his best, then we don't make it to finals. And if that happens." I met Kenzie's gaze, so calm, so warm. I grabbed her hand. "Then there's no way I'll get scouted."

Kenzie pulled away. "Oh." She crossed her arms over her chest and leaned against the doorframe.

But I could tell she didn't get it. "Kenzie." I sighed, reluctant to tell her this, but she needed to hear it from someone. "You're gorgeous, and believe me, a lot of guys at our school have noticed how you've"—I cleared my throat—"grown up over the past few years."

Kenzie gnawed on the side of her lip. "Okay ..."

"And your brother." I paused and rubbed the back of my neck. "Let's just say, he's made sure nobody messes with you."

Kenzie's green eyes met mine as she searched for more of an explanation. "What do you mean?" Her voice came out quavering.

I hated to bring this up, but she had to know. "Remember your date with Spencer Masterson last year?"

I was at Kenzie and Cory's house when Spencer showed up to ask her out ... on her first real date.

"Mmm hmm," she muttered. "He stood me up."

"Not exactly." I sighed, thinking back to what Cory did when he found out Spencer planned on taking Kenzie to Cedar Park lookout—only the biggest make-out spot in Cedar Oaks. "Your brother got to him."

"Got to him?" Confusion creased the corners of Kenzie's eyes. She sighed, her face lighting up in recognition. "The black eye?"

I nodded. "So you see, there's more riding on keeping that picture out of your brother's hands than you know."

"But why?" she asked.

"Don't you see?" I smiled. "With your dad gone, Cory treats you like a little kid and threatens those guys because he feels like he needs to protect you." I took a step closer to her and hushed my voice. "And when he finds out we've been ... kissing ... behind his back, then ..."

I looked to Kenzie's eyes and then to her trembling, full lips. "Then what are you gonna do?"

I swallowed down the lump in my throat, in disbelief of what I was about to say. "I need to bomb that quiz tomorrow."

"But what about that scout? He needs to see you play, Gavin."

I smiled. "There'll be other games," I said, an attempt to convince myself more than anybody else. But even I knew that wasn't true.

Kenzie put her foot down. Literally. She stomped her sneaker on the wood floor below. "This is ridiculous. You *will* take that quiz tomorrow. You'll earn that A. And you will play in Wednesday's game."

Even though I didn't exactly love being told what to do, I loved the authority in Kenzie's voice. I leaned my forehead against hers. "I can't, Kenzie."

Her voice trembled as the next words escaped her mouth. "Then this." She pulled away and spun her back to me. "Then this is over."

Just hearing her say those words ... *this is over* ... felt like a punch in the gut. "What?"

"Let Michael send that picture to Cory." Her eyes lit up. "Gosh ... my brother has to know I've had a crush on you like forever." She tucked a few pieces of hair behind her ear. "I'll tell him I misread some signals over tutoring, that I made a move at the party, and that you had nothing to do with the kiss ... the picture." She spun around and her eyes met mine. "He'll believe it."

I tugged the hem of Kenzie's shirt and pulled her toward me. "And then what?"

She shrugged. "And then we'll wait until the season is over." She stepped toward me and twined her fingers in mine. "Be together then."

I tugged on her sleeve and pulled her the rest of the way toward me. I bent over and kissed the top of her head, inhaling her floral shampoo. "That's two months away."

She rested her head on my chest. "Two months and you'll have a scholarship to Penn State."

I sighed and peered into her eyes, so bright and green, it was like looking into an evergreen forest. "Two months and I'll get to be with the girl I'm head over heels for."

Kenzie stood on her tiptoes and her hot breath tickled my ear as she whispered, "I've wanted to be with you for the past three years. What's another two months?" She pressed two warm lips to my cheek and then darted upstairs before I had the chance to say anything more.

That's settled then.

* * *

TWO HOURS LATER, I sat on my bed and re-read Act 3 of *A Midsummer Night's Dream*. I literally laughed out loud as Bottom, now adorned with the head of a donkey, proclaimed his love for Titania—queen of the fairies. Gosh, just four days ago, I wouldn't have had a chance at understanding this play. Just as I moved onto Scene 2, a text lit up my screen. My heartbeat caught in my throat at the name.

Cory: *So Kenzie just confessed her little crush on you. I'll hurt Michael for taking that picture.*

Phew. I tapped back a response.

Gavin: *I know. She took me off guard.*

Cory: *At least it was you and not some other jerk.*

I smiled inside. Maybe Cory would be okay with me and Kenz dating. And then the next text completely obliterated that thought.

Cory: *And if you kissed her, then we'd be done.*

I swallowed hard, contemplating whether or not to text the thoughts in my head. *Mackenzie is seventeen years old. She's not a kid. She can make her own decisions. Date who she wants.*
But that wasn't my place. The only person who could make that clear to Cory was Kenzie. Maybe it was a conversation I'd have with Cory in two months.
Only two months, I reminded myself.
I finished reading the rest of the act and then fell back on the pillow. That night I dreamt about kissing Kenzie Fair, and nobody stopped me.

CHAPTER 13

I walked into Fretz's class the next morning, and the first person I saw was Michael Sands. He dangled his iPhone from his fingertips. "To send, or not to send ..." he taunted. How poetic of him. I threw my backpack to the ground and took my seat, effectively ignoring the scowl on his face.

Without moving my head, I looked toward Gavin's seat and watched as his fingertips fidgeted with the edge of his notebook.

I pulled out my phone and tapped a message.

Kenzie: *Good luck on the quiz. Xo.*

"Alright, kiddos!" Fretz's voice boomed from the back of the room, so I shoved my phone into my back pocket. Fretz made his way down the row with a stack of papers —which I assumed were the quizzes—in his hands.

"Phones away. Pencils out." He smirked. "I hope you all read Act 3, because you have a quiz today."

Fake moans and groans sounded from just about everyone in the classroom. To be honest, we all knew about his pop-quiz well in advance.

Fretz slapped a quiz on Gavin's desk. "Good luck," he snarked. I'm sure he knew full well Gavin's soccer eligibility was riding on this grade.

I stole a look over my shoulder and mouthed "good luck" to him. Gavin peered at me from the corner of his eyes and curled his lips up in the corner. He winked. I shivered inside.

Ugh. Two months of this charade.

But it was worth it.

* * *

I MET Veda at Cafe Prose after school and filled her in on all things Gavin.

"And Cory has absolutely no idea?"

I shook my head, thinking back to last night when I'd confessed my undying love for Gavin to my brother, and the look of amusement that crossed his face when I told him how I'd kissed his best friend. My plan was working out perfectly.

I cupped my tea latte in my hands, warming them up. "He totally bought it." I batted my eyelashes. "I played the oblivious, awkward, nerdy, naive, little sister Cory thinks I am."

"So he saw the picture?"

I nodded. "I showed it to him." I leaned closer to Veda. "And Cory said he'll be taking care of Michael Sands after Wednesday's game."

"Yikes." Veda cringed. "I would not want to be on the receiving end of that."

I fidgeted in my seat as heat spread throughout my core. "Gavin said Cory has persuaded other guys in the past to stay away from me too ..."

Veda's eyes grew wide. "What?" She huffed. "That's so not okay."

"No kidding," I muttered. "But I'm not about to bring that up to him now."

Veda pursed her lips. "Smart. Then he'd know how *close* you and Gavin really are." Veda shimmied her shoulders and then suddenly stopped. Her cheeks flushed as the bell above she shop's door rang. "Don't turn around, Kenz," she demanded, just as I put the mug to my lips. But her saying that had the opposite effect. Really, anyone telling someone *not* to turn around is an invitation to do just that.

I choked on my latte as Claire Mullins and Emma Good walked through the door, droning on and on about the new cheerleader uniforms, while Gavin and Cory following closely behind. Just like a few days ago, I slunk down in my chair, hoping I'd somehow blend in with the leather material.

But obviously my purple tunic and black leggings weren't camouflage enough. I heard Claire's nasally voice echo across the room. "Aww, Gav. Your little crush is here."

Of course Cory told the most obnoxious girl in school about his sister's school-girl crush on her ex-boyfriend. I didn't even have to turn around to know Gavin stared at me. I felt the heat of embarrassment rise to my face. This was absolute torture.

Veda sent me a sympathetic stare.

"I think we should get out of here," I spat, getting up from the chair.

I didn't even glance in Gavin's direction. The door's bell jingled above as we stepped outside.

"Wanna ride home?" Veda asked, hopping into her car.

I only lived a five-block walk from the coffee shop. "I think I'll walk." The cool air would help clear my head anyway. I thought that two months of not *seeing*-seeing Gavin would be easy. But the way my stomach clenched at the sight of him just now, particularly the way he ignored me—told me I was wrong. These next two months would be torture.

Just as I rounded the corner of Maple, I heard my name. "Kenzie!"

I turned to see Gavin jogging toward me. He stopped two feet from me. "So I aced the quiz." He shoved his hands in his pockets and smiled. "Thanks to you."

I pushed a few leaves with the toe of my shoe. "That's great, Gavin."

"Look ..." he started. He pushed a hand through his hair. "I'm sorry about Claire." He gestured behind him. "Back there."

I couldn't help the tears from welling in the corners

of my eyes. My feelings for Gavin went deeper than I thought. "You're not ..." I couldn't finish the question.

"No way." Gavin stepped closer. "Cory invited Emma and Claire." His eyes met mine. "You know how I feel about you, Kenzie."

Gavin reached his hand toward me, but I backed away. "Someone might see."

But before I could take another step backward, Gavin's torso crashed into mine as his hands wrapped around my neck. "I don't care," he whispered. He leaned down and his lips met mine, gentle at first. But it was as if three years of crushing on me came together as his lips moved against mine, harder this time. He tasted like peppermint and chocolate and everything good and perfect I'd wanted for the past three years.

"Gavin?" a voice interrupted us.

My heart thudded against my chest. My brother's voice.

"Cory!" I yelped, jumping away from Gavin. I put a finger to my tingling lips while Cory clenched and unclenched his jaw.

"What's going on here, Gav?" Cory asked.

Gavin put his hands up as if in surrender. "Nothing," he said.

Cory rushed toward Gavin and grabbed his jacket—two fistfuls of material balled in his hands.

"Stop it, Cory!" I yelled, stepping in between the two friends. "It's not what you think."

Cory let go of the material as his chest heaved up and down, up and down. His eyes met mine. "Then what is it,

Kenzie? Are you going to tell me *you* made the move again?" Cory stomped a foot on the sidewalk. "How long has this actually been going on?"

Gavin stepped forward. "Just a few days." He put a hand on Cory's shoulder. "But I've had feelings for Kenzie for a long time."

"What?" Cory slapped Gavin's hand away. "What is that supposed to mean?" He pushed a finger into Gavin's chest. Just as Gavin opened his mouth to say more, Cory spoke. "You stay away from her," he said through clenched teeth. "Stay away from me. Stay away from all of us."

"That's not fair!" I yelled at my brother.

I turned toward Gavin. "Please, just leave." The words came out harsher than I'd intended. Gavin ran a hand through his hair and stepped away, still facing me.

"You heard her," Cory spat.

Gavin's eyes searched mine. "Please," I repeated. This was something my brother and I needed to discuss. Gavin nodded and then jogged to his Jeep. I chewed on the side of my cheek when he didn't turn around.

"What were you thinking, Kenzie?" Cory asked.

"I just—."

"Stop it." Cory's breath came out in short bursts. "I told Dad I'd protect you and that includes protecting you from Gavin."

I felt a tear trickle down my cheek. "But he's your best friend, Cory," I protested.

Cory grimaced. "And I think that makes it even worse."

I stepped toward my brother. "Worse, how?" I threw two hands in the air. "Worse than Michael Sands?" I narrowed my eyes at him, ignoring the chill that suddenly swept through the air. "Worse than a brother who's pushed everyone away from me?"

Cory rolled his eyes. "Whatever, Kenz."

"Not whatever." I pointed a finger at his chest. "I know about your threats." Cory's head snapped toward me, and I continued. "Spencer's black eye ring a bell?"

A flicker of recognition crossed his face. "He wouldn't have been good for you, Kenz. I know it."

"*You* know it? I've had enough of this. Enough of you baby-ing me." It was like three years of anger from being babied, from being *protected* came to a head. "When are you going to realize I'm not a little kid anymore, Cory?" I yelled, tears welling in the corners of my eyes. I wiped them with the back of my hand and spoke louder, mustering more power and authority than ever before. "I can make my own decisions, so you can either stop treating me like a child or stay out of my life," I spat. "The decision's yours."

I spun on my heels and stomped away, my entire body shaking as I jogged the rest of the way home, realizing in a matter of minutes, my first semi-relationship was over, and the tenuous relationship I'd had with my brother might be gone as well.

CHAPTER 14

I got to my room and threw my body on the purple and white striped comforter. For the past seventeen years, I'd been in Cory's shadow, and finally ... finally, I'd stood up to him. Although a part of me felt broken, the other part of me felt relieved.

But what am I going to do about Gavin?

Everything was ruined. Sure, he'd play in Wednesday's game, but if they lost, I'd feel responsible for it. I'd texted him three times in the past two hours, and nothing. I pushed a tear from my cheek and then grabbed a copy of *Shakespeare's Greatest Works* from my nightstand. I opened up to my favorite play—*Romeo and Juliet*.

When I was in middle school, every night before bed, Dad and I would read a scene. Yeah, cliché love story. But it was so much more than that—family rivalries, themes of loyalty, friendship, betrayal. And right now, the irony wasn't lost on me. The last thing I needed was a play about forbidden love to cheer me up. I opened up to Act 2, Scene 2, and just as I began reading, I heard a fist knock on my bedroom door.

"Kenzie?" my brother's voice asked.

"I'm busy." I flipped to my favorite monologue.

Cory knocked twice more. "Please let me in."

I sighed and placed a bookmark in the play. "I said I'm busy." No matter how angry I was, or how much I wanted to hate my brother, he was my brother. "Fine," I huffed. I sat up straight and pushed my book to the side of the bed.

Cory stood in the doorway, awkwardly leaning on the frame. He gestured toward the book. "You know they both die at the end?"

I looked at him with a stoic, completely unamused expression on my face. "Well their families did forbid them from being together ..."

"Touché," Cory noted.

He stepped into my room and glanced around, from the picture of the four of us—Mom, Dad, Cory, and me one summer in Cape May—to the filled bookshelf next to my desk. "Can I sit?" He gestured to the edge of my bed.

I shrugged and played with the fraying ends of my sweatshirt sleeves.

The bed sunk in where Cory sat. He turned his torso to face me. "Look, Kenzie. I'm sorry."

I shrugged. "About what exactly?" I narrowed my eyes. "Freaking out on me? Freaking out on your best friend? Being a jerk? Meddling in my life?"

Cory fidgeted with his hands. "About all of it." He sighed. "After Dad died ..." Cory looked toward the window and pulled his lips to the side. His eyes met mine, and there were tears in the corners. "I told myself I'd make sure nothing bad would happen to you."

"Okay ..."

"And I think I took that to the extreme."

"Yeah." I sat up straighter and locked eyes with Cory. "Scaring guys away from me goes a bit beyond extreme."

"It does." He chuckled, and the tension in the air thinned out.

Cory's eyes met mine. "But Gavin, Kenz?" He shrugged. "He's my best friend."

"What?" I nudged his shoulder. "You think I'm gonna steal him away from you?"

Cory smiled weakly. "It's just ... after Dad ... I noticed how much Gavin helped out. Helped you and Mom while I just sat back and did nothing."

"You were hurting, Cory. Grieving, too."

Cory shook his head from side to side and a blond piece of hair fell in front of his green eyes—eyes that matched mine, and had matched Dad's, in every way. "Yeah, but I wasn't there enough," he admitted. "I didn't want Gavin to replace ..." Cory's voice trailed off.

Suddenly, it all clicked into place. The only reason Cory didn't want me with Gavin was because of jealousy. Was my overly confident, popular brother admitting his insecurities to his *little* sister? I reached out a hand and placed it on my brother's. "Cory, nobody could replace you."

He nodded his head. "Thanks, Kenzie." He took a deep breath and then stood. "And for the record, I haven't seen you as an annoying little sister for a while."

"Mmm hmmm." His actions over the previous years said otherwise, but I had to commend his effort. "But can you agree to let me date whomever I'd like?"

"I won't promise that." Cory shrugged. "But I'll try."

I nodded. "And I'll take that."

Cory inhaled and stood. "So you really like him, huh?"

I pushed my tongue to the side of my cheek, willing the tears to stay put. "Mmm hmm. For a while actually," I admitted.

Cory moved across the room, reached the door, and just as he stepped into the hallway, he turned around. "But if Gavin hurts you, Kenzie, so help me ..."

"About that ..." I chewed on my lip. "After you went ballistic on him, I'm not so sure he'll want to see me anytime soon."

Cory shrugged. "We'll see," he said coolly and then stepped into the hall, disappearing around the corner.

I got up from my bed and looked in the dresser mirror. I sighed at the reflection looking back. I dabbed on some concealer Veda'd given me after the party the other night, hiding the pink pouches under my eyes, and I pinched my cheeks for color. I braided the front pieces of hair together and then pinned them behind my ear. "You do just fine without a boy," I reminded myself. I'd been fine with my best friend and my books for the past sixteen and a half years, after all. But with Gavin, I felt more than fine.

Suddenly, the doorbell rang.

"Can you get that?" Cory's voice echoed down the hallway.

And yet my brother is still telling me what to do.

I clomped down the steps and reached the front door. As soon as I touched the knob though, butterflies began flittering around my stomach, sensing who was on the other side.

I opened the door and smiled, my hunch right.

"Hi, Gavin," I wisped out. He looked cute, dressed in jeans, a fitted green shirt and his varsity jacket. His eyes shined under the porch light, and the wind carried the pine and clove scent of his soap through the air, filling my nose.

"Hey, Kenzie." Gavin ran a hand across the back of his neck. "So can we talk?"

I swallowed as a rock dropped in the pit of my stomach. *Can we talk?* The words that anyone dreads to hear. I nodded slightly. "Sure." I grabbed my coat and met him on the porch.

Gavin shoved his hands in his pockets. "So, your brother stopped by a little while ago."

I groaned. "Please don't tell me he hit you."

Gavin pointed to his face, clear of bruises. "No." He smirked. "We just talked about a few things."

I wrapped my coat tighter around my torso. "Like what?"

Gavin leaned against the railing. "Soccer, school …"

His voice trailed off and part of his neck bulged out as he swallowed. "You." His eyes met mine.

I stepped closer as the wind whipped strands of blond hair around my face. "Is that so?"

"I just had to explain a few things to him." Gavin reached out a hand and brushed a strand of hair from my cheek.

"Is that so?" I asked again, feeling warmth spread across my cheeks.

Gavin nodded. He inched closer to me, his hand leaving my face and finding my own hand.

I moved closer to him. "And what did you have to explain?"

"Cory needed to know what I feel ..." Gavin looked to the ground and then looked back up, his blue eyes meeting mine. "What I've felt for a while now."

The next question came out a whisper. "And what's that?"

Gavin ran his fingertips up my arm, over my shoulder, and under my chin, tilting my head slightly toward him. "That I love you." His face inched toward mine. "That I've been in love with you for a while now."

At those words, it felt as if the wind was knocked out of me. I stood higher on my toes and met his gaze.

Gavin bent down and wrapped his hands around my neck. He nudged my head the rest of the way forward until our mouths met. The kiss was gentle and it made me forget about the frigid air surrounding us as it warmed me to the core.

Gavin pulled away, his eyes meeting mine.

This was the moment I'd been waiting for for the past three years. Gavin leaned forward, and I closed my eyes as he kissed my forehead and then my cheeks and then my nose. Before his lips went to mine once more, I finally responded. "I love you too, Gavin."

EPILOGUE

I grabbed my graduation cap from the entryway table at Kenzie's house and yelled up the stairs. "You about ready?"

"Coming!" Kenzie called. I looked to the top of the stairs where Kenzie stood, and my breath hitched in my throat.

I'm the luckiest guy in the world.

Kenzie wore a light blue dress, the hem falling a few inches above her knees and the breezy cotton material hugged her curves. Her hair had grown longer over the past six months, and now fell in soft curls two inches below her shoulders. I grabbed Kenzie's hand when she got to the bottom of the stairs and spun her in a circle—drinking in her beauty—from her strappy sandals, to the top of her head with the signature braid tucked behind her ear. "You look gorgeous." I smiled, in disbelief she was my girlfriend.

I kissed her cheek and then she pulled back. Kenzie

squinted her eyes and appraised me. "Not so bad yourself, college boy."

I put a finger in the air. "Not quite yet."

"You coming, Cory?" I called up to my best friend.

Cory yelled from his bedroom, and his voice echoed down the stairs and through the foyer. "Mom and I will meet you guys there."

Kenzie shrugged and slipped her hand in mine. "Shall we?"

We hopped in my Jeep and headed to my graduation ceremony.

I couldn't believe how quickly the past six months had gone by. After I admitted my love for Kenzie, we'd been practically inseparable. Although it took Cory a while to come around to the idea of his best friend dating his sister, eventually the shock wore off. A playoff win followed by winning the championship game didn't hurt either.

Because of those games, both Cory and I got scouted and then received offers from our number-one college —Penn State.

Kenzie turned toward me and her lips curled up in a smile that made my heart beat faster in my chest. Like she read my mind about Penn State, she spoke. "Only a two-hour drive." She looked out the window.

"Mmm hmm," I muttered. "And I'll see you at least twice a month." I reached over and rested my hand on her knee.

Kenzie nodded her head and then stared ahead until we reached Cedar Oaks' stadium. Once we arrived I ran around to Kenzie's side of the Jeep and rested my hands on each side of her hips, lifting her down from the car. Her feet landed on the ground, with her body still pressed to mine. I inhaled her flowery shampoo and then kissed the top of her head. "You know I'm the luckiest guy in the world," I said aloud this time.

Kenzie's cheeks turned a light shade of pink at my compliment. "You might have mentioned that before." She raised her eyebrow, stood on her tiptoes, and pressed two lips to my cheek.

I peered into her emerald eyes. "You know..." I pointed to Kenzie and then back to me. "This never would have happened without Mr. Fretz."

Kenzie threw her head back and laughed. "Or if you were a little better in English," she teased.

I lifted a hand to her neck and rubbed the hollow spot just under her collarbone. "I'm just glad it did happen."

Kenzie swallowed and played with the hair that curled just behind my ears. "I am too." She pulled her mouth to the side. "But what about—."

I put a finger to her lips, stopping her from saying more. She wanted to continue the conversation from earlier. But there was no point.

"I am madly in love with my best friend's sister." I paused and peered into Kenzie's eyes. "With all my heart." I grabbed her hand and pushed it to my chest, wondering if she could feel the thrumming within it.

Kenzie sighed. "And you know I'm in love with you."

I loved Kenzie Fair, and she loved me. That was a fact.

I tugged on her purse string, pulling her toward me. She bit the side of her lip, my signal to lean in closer. She tilted her head to the side and a jolt of electricity coursed through me as our lips met, just as it did the first time we kissed. As the kiss deepened, with her fingers twined in my hair, I was certain of one thing.

Sure, Kenzie and I had our weekends, our breaks, our summers together. But I knew in my heart, we had the rest of our lives together too.

*** * ***

WANT MORE SHORT, SWEET, SWOON-WORTHY ROMANCE? GRAB ANOTHER BOOK BY JULIET BARDSLEY!

WANT MORE ROMANCE? JOIN JULIET'S READER'S CLUB AND NEVER MISS A NEW RELEASE OR FUN GIVEAWAYS!

And check out some other Snowy Wings Publishing sweet romance titles ...

ACKNOWLEDGMENTS

Although I've been a children's book author for years, I've always loved all things romantic and cozy, and so a few months ago I decided to venture into writing sweet and swoon-worthy romance for adults and young adults. I'm excited to start this journey into a new genre and have a few people to thank for the push.

Thank you to my editor for helping shape up this book — especially my love of commas and unnecessary speaker tags.

Thanks to my readers, current and future for coming back to my words.

A HUGE thanks to my family.

And the biggest thanks of all goes to my husband, Eddie. Thank you for supporting me in this new venture and urging me to keep pursuing my writing dream, even when the stressors of life overwhelm me. You are amazing and our love inspires me to write these books. I love you and B to the moon and back.

ABOUT THE AUTHOR

Juliet Bardsley is an author of romance that's short, sweet, and swoon-worthy. When she's not writing, Juliet can be found spending time with her family, snuggling under a blanket watching Hallmark movies, or reading anything sweet and cozy. To be notified when she has a new release, giveaways, and other sweet goodies, please sign up for her newsletter.